JESSICA BECK

THE DONUT MYSTERIES, BOOK 23

RASPBERRY REVENGE

MYS
Pbk

The First Time Ever Published!

The 23rd Donut Mystery.

Jessica Beck is the *New York Times* Bestselling Author of the Donut Mysteries, the Classic Diner Mysteries, the Ghost Cat Cozy Mysteries, and the Cast Iron Cooking Mysteries.

To my spouse and my daughter,
For all of the reasons that matter.

When Mayor George Morris's chief rival, Harley Boggess, is found murdered while sitting behind the mayor's desk in City Hall, it looks as though George may have dispatched his competition permanently. When the mayor goes missing immediately afterward, things appear to be even worse, and it's up to Suzanne, her mother, and Grace to work together to uncover who really killed the councilman before the mayor's future—and his freedom—are extinguished forever.

CHAPTER 1

"**G**EORGE, ARE YOU IN HERE?" I asked as I knocked on the mayor's office door again, quite a bit louder this time, as I balanced a bag of donuts and a cup of coffee with my other hand.

There was still no response from inside.

I'd just finished my workday at Donut Hearts, my shop located in the heart of April Springs, North Carolina. The George I was visiting at the moment was none other than George Morris, the mayor of our quaint little town and a good friend of mine. George hadn't been by the donut shop for at least a week, which was out of character for him, so I'd decided to take matters into my own hands and pay him a visit. On my way out the door of the donut shop, I'd grabbed a few cake donuts and some coffee and headed over to his office.

Only it appeared that the mayor wasn't there. "Ready or not, I'm coming in," I said as I turned the handle and opened the door. The mayor's high-backed chair was turned toward the window, where I knew from experience he could see the clock and most of our town square. The Christmas decorations had been down for a month, and the landscape had a gray sameness to it that made me wish for snow, or at the very least, the early arrival of spring. Anything would be a nice change from the uniform palette we were currently living in.

I put the bag of donuts and the coffee down on the edge of

his desk, and then on a whim, I walked around and looked out the window to take in the view.

It still amazes me that I didn't notice the body right away, but I was focused on the sights outside, and it wasn't until I turned around that I realized that I wasn't alone.

If you could call being in the same room with a dead body having company.

CHAPTER 2

I LEANED OVER THE PALE CORPSE to check for a pulse and found his skin cold to the touch. The man had eaten something loaded with onions for his last meal, based on the smell that lingered around him. I doubted that it would have been his first choice of final foods, but then again, he probably wasn't aware that his end had been in sight. It didn't take a medical examiner to determine that he had been dead for quite some time, especially since there was a wickedly sharp letter opener sticking in his chest buried almost all the way to the handle. Clearly there was nothing I could do for him, so I reached for my cellphone and dialed my husband's number automatically. After all, Jake was the acting chief of police, and besides, who else would I call at a time like that? Unfortunately, it went straight to voicemail, and I knew that I couldn't exactly hang around and wait for him to call me back, so I hung up and dialed 911 instead.

"There's a dead body in the mayor's office," I said breathlessly the moment I got an answer.

"George Morris is dead?" the dispatcher asked me in disbelief.

"Not that I know of. Why, do you know something I don't?"

"Who is this?" the man asked shrilly. I couldn't blame him for his reaction. I doubted that he'd dealt with many murders in the past, though we'd seemed to have had more than our fair share around town over the last few years.

"It's Suzanne Hart, your boss's wife. I just came by the

mayor's office to bring him some coffee and donuts, and I found a dead body instead."

"If it's not the mayor, then who is it?"

It was a logical question, though it felt as though we were wasting time to me, but clearly the officer in the chair was having trouble catching up. "It's Harley Boggess," I said. "It appears that someone has stabbed him in the heart with the mayor's letter opener." From the look of things, the town councilman, who also happened to be George's chief nemesis in town politics, wasn't going to be bothering the mayor anymore.

At least that's what I thought at the time.

CHAPTER 3

"**S**UZANNE, ARE YOU OKAY?" JAKE asked me the moment he arrived, glancing my way before he leaned over to get a closer look at Harley's body. I nodded as he started his inspection, and he quickly arrived at the same conclusion that I had. Only after Jake was satisfied with what he'd seen did he offer me comfort by hugging me briefly before any of his deputies arrived on the scene. I knew that Jake was an exemplary officer of the law, but at that moment I needed him more as my husband than a police chief, so I was happy for the solace, no matter how brief, I received.

"I thought it was George at first," I said as Stephen Grant—Jake's second in command and my best friend, Grace Gauge's, boyfriend—started taking video of the body and its surroundings.

"They do look a little bit alike," Jake said as he gazed down at the dead body, "but don't tell George I said that. Where is the mayor, anyway? Do you know?"

"I have no idea. I thought he was here," I said. I pointed to the coffee and the bag of donuts still on the desk. "When he didn't answer my knock, I figured that he might be lost in thought, so I came on in. I brought him some goodies as a treat, but I found Harley instead."

"Don't worry about George. We'll track him down," Jake said reassuringly.

"Do you think he might be dead, too?" I asked hesitantly.

I hadn't been able to get the 911 dispatcher's comment out of my head.

"What? No. Of course not. This isn't a coup for power, and I doubt that it's a case of mistaken identity. I'm sure that George is just fine, wherever he is."

"I know that you're probably right, but I'll feel a lot better once I see him again."

"Tell me what happened one more time," Jake asked me softly.

"I already told you everything I did and saw from the second I arrived twice already," I protested.

"Once more, and then I'll leave you alone," Jake said with a reassuring smile.

"I certainly hope not." I did as he asked, recounting the same story again.

Jake seemed satisfied, and as he closed his handheld notebook after checking his notes, he asked, "Should I call Grace or your mother for you?"

"No. Why would you want to do that?"

"I just thought you might be able to use a little support right now," he said.

"That's what I've got you for," I said as I touched his shoulder lightly.

"Suzanne, I'll do all that I can, but you've got to realize that I can't focus all of my attention on you this second."

"I know that." It was part of what it meant to have a husband in law enforcement, and I'd grown used to the idea that Jake couldn't always be there for me. "Grace is out of town for a conference."

"Then your mother it is," Jake said. Before I could stop him, he dialed her number and invited her to join us at the mayor's office as soon as possible without revealing a single detail as to why. Only Jake could have gotten away with that, but my mother had a soft spot in her heart for him; I sometimes wondered if she preferred him over me. I wasn't jealous, though. It was heartwarming to see how she'd embraced my second husband, especially given the relationship she'd had with my first one. Momma and Max had gotten along like cats and dogs, so it was a nice change of pace to see the way she doted on my husband.

Three minutes after Jake called her, my mother appeared in the outer office, clamoring to get in. Jake had stationed a deputy outside, but it wasn't enough to keep my mother at bay, especially not when there might be something wrong with her cub.

"I'd better go out there before she causes a riot," I said with a wry smile.

"That's a good idea. I'd hate to see one of my people going to the hospital. I'll call you the second we find George."

"Thanks," I said, and then I went out and greeted my mother.

After I told her that I'd found Harley Boggess's dead body in the mayor's chair, Momma said, "Thank the dear Lord above that you're all right, child," as she wrapped me in her arms. I was substantially taller than she was, and quite a bit heavier, but I instantly felt like a little kid again as I felt myself give in to her embrace. "Are you all right, Suzanne?" she asked as she reached up and stroked my hair.

"I'm fine, Momma," I told her in a soft voice, though a few tears racing down my cheeks testified that I was lying. It was just hitting me that I'd found a dead body, and I wasn't anywhere near hardened enough by my experiences in the past to just shake it off. I was a donut maker, after all, not a cop who might reasonably expect to find death around every corner. Harley Boggess was dead, but not only that, someone had clearly chosen to take his life from him. That shook me to the core of my being, no matter how brave I pretended to be at times.

Momma kept stroking my hair and talking in her soothing voice that was reserved for the most trying of times. "Does George know what's happening?" she asked softly.

"We can't find him!" I said, the uncertainty of his fate thick in my voice.

"Don't worry. I'm sure that he'll turn up soon. Jake will be able to track him down if anyone can," Momma said, and then she pulled away a little so that she could look me directly in the eye. She must have been troubled by what she saw. "Let's get you home."

"If it's all the same to you, I don't want to be around anybody else right now. It's nothing against Phillip at all," I said, quickly mentioning her husband's name.

"I didn't mean my home; I meant yours," she said. I currently lived with Jake in the cottage I'd grown up in, but I'd shared it with Momma before she'd married Phillip and moved out, turning the place over to me. It truly was home, since I'd lived there my entire life except for college and my ill-fated first marriage to Max.

"That sounds great," I said as I allowed her to lead me outside to her car.

"Where's your Jeep?" she asked as she looked around.

"It's still at the donut shop. It's so close that I decided to walk over."

"Well, don't worry about that. We'll pick it up later." We got into Momma's car and drove the short distance to the cottage, past the donut shop, the Boxcar Grill, the park, and Grace's home, until we made it home. Walking through the front door with my mother felt as natural as it could be, something I desperately needed at the moment. Any normalcy in a world turned upside down was most welcome. "I'll just start a fire, and then we can sit together and watch it until you feel better," Momma said.

I was in no mood to protest, especially since her plan sounded ideal to me. Once Momma got me settled in on the couch, wrapped in a blanket and facing the nascent flames, she asked, "Should I make us some hot chocolate?"

"Just stay with me for a bit," I asked as I reached out a hand for her.

"Of course," Momma said as she settled in beside me. I shared my blanket with her, and we sat there together in comfortable silence, watching the flames, each of us left to our own thoughts.

The quiet time was nice while it lasted, but of course, it was interrupted long before I was ready to deal with the outside world. There was a sudden knock at the door, pulling Momma and me both out of our comfortable silence.

"Is there any chance if we don't answer, they'll just go away?" I asked her softly.

"As much as we'd like to sometimes, we can't hide from the world, Suzanne," Momma said, getting in another one of the life lessons she'd raised me on. I didn't know how to remind her that I was a grown woman without hurting her feelings, and besides, her instincts were probably spot on. Even though I was an adult, I still managed to do stupid things on occasion that baffled me. Was I ever going to grow up? Probably not completely, if I was being honest with myself.

She started to get up, but I said, "Stay there. I'll answer it."

"You don't have to do that," Momma said gently.

"I know, but you're right. I need to see who's there." When I opened the door, I was thrilled to see Grace Gauge standing there, replete in full business attire. "Grace, what are you doing here? I thought you were out of town at a conference."

"I was, but when I heard what happened over the radio, I called Stephen immediately, and he gave me all of the details. After that, I came straight here," she said as she hugged me fiercely. "How horrible it must have been for you to find Harley's body like that."

"It was a bit of a shock," I admitted after we broke our hug. "Listen, I appreciate the gesture, but I don't want you getting in trouble because of me."

"No worries. I told them that my grandmother was sick," she said with a smile. "So, how are you feeling, Granny?"

"I'm still a little shaky, to be honest with you," I said with a weak grin. "Come on in."

"I don't mean to intrude," Grace said when she spotted my mother hovering in the background. Grace offered her a smile and took a step back.

"Nonsense. You know that you are always welcome here, Grace," Momma said before adding quickly, "At least I assume so. After all, this isn't my cottage anymore. It's Suzanne's, so ultimately, it's up to her."

It was fun watching my mother squirm a little, and for a moment, it took my mind off what was going on. "Momma's right. Come on in."

"While you two girls are catching up, I'll go make that hot chocolate I promised you earlier," she said. After two steps toward the kitchen, she turned to Grace. "If cocoa is all right with you, that is."

"All right? It sounds spectacular," Grace said as she rubbed her hands together. "It's freezing out there."

Once Momma was in the kitchen, Grace and I sat on the couch and faced the flames. "Now tell me everything, Suzanne. You know how men are. Stephen gave me the facts, but he left out all of the important details. How bad was it?"

"Well, it wasn't good," I said. "Finding the body was hard, but right now I'm more worried about George than anything else."

"What about him?" she asked me, clearly alarmed by my statement. "Was he hurt during the attack?"

"Do you mean that you haven't heard?"

"Nobody said anything to me about George, though Stephen did tell me that you found Harley's body in City Hall."

"Actually, he was in George's chair," I said, "and what's worse, George is missing."

"He's missing? What do you mean?"

"I don't know how else to say it. No one knows where he is, and I'm worried about him, Grace."

"You honestly don't think George had anything to do with what happened to Harley, do you?"

"Of course not," I said, perhaps protesting a little too loudly.

"Me, either, but we both know that those two men couldn't stand each other, and George never made any apologies for it," Grace said.

"You don't have to remind me," I said, trying to keep the angst out of my voice. "I just wish he were here to tell us his side of things."

"Is Jake out looking for him? I hope he doesn't put out an APB for him."

"I don't think he will. All-points bulletins are just for guilty people, aren't they?"

"I have no idea how it works, but I'd hate to see George's name tarnished because of this," Grace said.

My cellphone rang, and I thought about ignoring it for one second, but then I realized it might be Jake or, even better, the mayor himself.

My first instinct had been correct; it was my husband.

"Did you find him?" I asked Jake before he had a chance to get a word out.

"No, but we have a little more information now than we had before."

"What is it? Don't keep me hanging like this, Jake! George is my friend."

"I know that," my husband said calmly. "That's why you're getting this call, though I probably shouldn't be disclosing any of this information to you."

"I won't share what you tell me in confidence with anyone," I said.

"Not even Grace or your mother?" Jake asked.

I didn't know how to answer that, so I didn't.

After a moment of silence, he continued. "Just don't broadcast it to the world, okay? The word will get out soon enough without the three of you talking to anyone else about it."

"Something happened to him, didn't it?" I asked, a knot of fear growing in my gut. I didn't know what I'd do without my friend George. Over the years, he'd become someone special to me, and the thought of living without him in my life was almost too much to take.

"Not that we know of."

"I thought you said that you had news," I said.

"Suzanne, if you'd take a deep breath and let me talk for a change, you'll hear it." He was getting frustrated with me, and honestly, I couldn't blame him.

I suddenly realized that he had a valid point. I wasn't being fair to my husband. "I'm sorry. You're right."

"No, I'm not," Jake said, his voice revealing his disappointment in himself. "You have every reason to be upset about the situation. I'm worried about George, too. Finding Harley dead in George's chair doesn't look good, and him running away doesn't help matters any."

"How do we know that he's really on the run? George might not even know about what happened to Harley," I reminded him.

"I suppose it's possible."

"What is it, Jake? What are you not telling me?"

He sighed heavily before he spoke, and when he did finally talk, his voice was heavy and sad. "We just got an anonymous tip that the mayor was spotted driving out of town like it was on fire not ten minutes before you found Harley's body," Jake said.

"That could mean anything," I said haltingly.

"It could," Jake agreed.

"But you think it's significant, don't you?"

"Suzanne, it's too early to know what to think at this point. I just wanted to keep you informed."

"Thanks. I appreciate that. I love you."

"I love you, too. I'll let you know if I hear anything else."

"I'll be waiting," I said. When I finished my call, I bit my lower lip. George couldn't have done it.

Right?

CHAPTER 4

A FTER A MOMENT OF SILENCE, Grace asked me, "What was that all about, Suzanne?" just as Momma walked back into the room carrying a tray loaded with three mugs of hot chocolate.

"I might as well tell you both at once, but it's not supposed to go beyond this room. Are we agreed?"

"I understand. I'll wait in the kitchen," Momma said as she put the tray down and turned to leave.

"Don't you want to know what Jake just told me?"

"Not if I can't share the news with my husband," Momma said. "Go on. Tell Grace about it. It's fine."

"Okay, I'm going to make an executive decision. You may tell Phillip, but ask him not to say anything to anyone else," I said, hoping that the circle of news didn't extend any further.

"I can do that," Momma said as she grabbed a mug and settled in on a nearby chair.

"Someone called in a tip about George," I said. "He was seen leaving town in a hurry not long before I found Harley's body."

"That doesn't necessarily mean that he's responsible for the murder," Momma said.

"I know that, and more importantly, so does Jake. It doesn't help matters though, does it?"

"The question is what are we going to do about it?" Grace asked me.

"What do you mean?" I asked.

14

"Suzanne, even if George has a perfectly reasonable explanation for running away, he's still going to look guilty until Harley Boggess's real killer is found."

"Are you saying that we should start investigating the murder even before Jake finds George?"

"That's exactly what I'm saying," Grace said.

I looked at Momma, expecting her to disapprove. Instead, I saw that she was nodding. "She's right, Suzanne. Even the appearance of guilt is going to ruin George's chances of ever being reelected again."

"Momma, there's a great deal more at stake than an election here," I reminded her.

"I fully realize that, but George's political life is extremely important to him. We need to find Harley's killer before folks accept the fact, whether it's true or not, that George is a killer and that he can't be trusted."

"We?" I asked her.

"Why not? I've helped you before. Why shouldn't the three of us work together on this? After all, I knew Harley better than either one of you, and I have access to more people who associated with him than you two ever would, if you'll forgive me for saying it. You both need me on this case, Suzanne."

I wished that I could tell her that she was wrong, but I knew in my heart that she wasn't. Harley had been a businessman who moved in my mother's circles. Many of those folks wouldn't talk to Grace or me unless my mother was involved as well. I turned to Grace. "What do you think?"

"It's your call, but as far as I'm concerned, we can use all of the help we can get on this one."

Momma nodded. "Then it's settled. The three of us are going to solve this case together."

"What is your husband going to think about us doing this?" I asked my mother.

"You let me worry about that. More importantly, what is *yours* going to think?" she countered.

"Jake might not be happy about it, but he'll find a way to live with it," I answered.

"As will my husband," Momma said.

Grace grinned. "Don't look at me. Stephen already knows that I'm going to do what pleases me; as a matter of fact, I think that's one of the things he loves most about me."

"Why wouldn't he?" Momma asked as she smiled at Grace. "You're quite a loveable young lady."

"Okay then, it's settled. It's the three of us against one cold-blooded killer," I said.

"The poor soul doesn't stand a chance," Momma said.

"Let's hope you're right," I answered.

I'd worked with Momma before, though Grace was usually my sole partner in my investigations. When we'd first started digging into murder, George had helped us, but he wasn't in any position to offer assistance on this particular case, even if we did manage to track him down. Momma, Grace, and I had never worked together on a murder case, and I wasn't sure how it was going to go.

There was only one way to find out, though.

It was time to start looking into Harley Boggess's murder.

I just hoped that George showed up sooner rather than later.

We had enough complications to deal with as it was.

"So, where shall we start?" Momma asked us once we got settled in.

"First we need to gather information," I said.

"About?"

"Harley Boggess's life and times," I answered. "We need to know who disliked him enough to kill him, and we have to start from scratch."

"Not necessarily," Momma replied.

"Dot, do you know something we don't?" Grace asked her.

"I've done business with Harley enough to know some things about him that others may not be privy to," Momma answered.

"Such as?" I asked.

"For one thing, he and his business partner have been talking about dissolving their association for the past two months," she answered. "From what I understand, there's a good bit of acrimony there."

"If they've been threatening to break up their partnership for months, then why kill him now?" Grace asked.

"The word out in the business world is that Curtis Daniels was getting fed up with the delaying tactics; Harley was dragging his feet, trying to extort more than his share of what their company was really worth."

"How did you hear about that?" I asked her. "I haven't heard anything about it."

"It could be because we travel in different circles, Suzanne."

"I get it. I know the common man, and you're more acquainted with the elite of April Springs, is that it?" I didn't much care for the implication. After all, my customers came in all shapes, sizes, colors, and socioeconomic levels.

"Don't take offense. One is no better or worse than the other. It's simply that the groups we have dealings with on a regular basis are different. If you don't mind, I'd like to speak with Curtis myself."

"Sure, but not alone, though," I said forcefully. "That's one of our hard-and-fast rules, Momma. Unless it has to be done solo, and I mean that's the *only* way we get the information, we work in teams."

"Very well. You both may go with me, as long as I'm allowed to do the majority of the talking."

Momma was being herself, taking over at the slightest

opportunity, but I had to stop that before we got in too deep. "Sorry, but you don't get to make the rules here, Momma. We have to decide what's best together."

"I wasn't trying to steamroll either one of you," she said, and then she chuckled softly. "Well, perhaps that's not entirely true, but I see your point. We'll go together."

"Sorry, but that's not going to work, either," Grace said reluctantly.

I was nearly as surprised as Momma was by the statement. "Grace, are you quitting just because there are three of us?"

"Of course not. I just know that some folks feel reticent about speaking with us when there are only two people asking questions. How do you think they'll react if there are three of us?"

"What are we going to do?" I asked, seeing her point immediately.

"I suppose I can drop out of the group if it will make your investigation easier," Momma said magnanimously.

"You can't. We need you," I told her, and then I turned to Grace. "What do you suggest?"

"We divide and conquer," Grace replied.

"I meant what I said when I just told Momma that I don't like the idea of any of us working alone," I reminded her.

"Neither do I. When Dot gets a lead, you two can pursue it. When it's someone we come up with, the two of us ask questions. It means that you'll be there every step of the way, but it's the only way I see this working."

I nodded. It made perfect sense, but I was still glad that I wasn't the one who had suggested it. It meant that I was in the middle of every part of our investigation, which was exactly where I wanted to be, but by its very nature, the arrangement meant that Momma and Grace would each see only parts of the whole puzzle.

"Suzanne, I think that's perfect, but you're going to need to make a concerted effort in keeping us both informed," Momma said.

"I can do that," I said. "So, who do we tackle first?" I wasn't about to make one of them sit on the sidelines. They were going to have to work that out between themselves.

"I'm still free to make some telephone calls by myself, am I not?" Momma asked.

"Of course," I said.

"Then I will stay here and reach out to a few folks who might have the information we're looking for. In the meantime, you two girls can go out and see what the word is on the street."

"We're not exactly going to poll random people about who might have killed Harley," I said.

"I wasn't being literal," she said. "Now, shoo, you two. Shall we meet back here in an hour?"

"Let's make it ninety minutes," I said.

"And at the Boxcar Grill," Grace added. "What can I say? I know I'll be hungry by then."

"Very well," Momma said. "Now off you go."

Grace and I were out on my front porch when I turned and asked her, "Are we being railroaded here?"

"Your mother has a strong personality," Grace replied with a smile. "That explains where you must have gotten it."

I laughed. "I'd smack you if it weren't true. So, who do we go after first?"

"I don't care, but the first thing I'm going to do is go home and change. I'm not wearing a suit during these interviews."

"I don't know," I said as I pretended to appraise her outfit. "You kind of class our team up."

"I believe we'll still be classy enough even after I change," she said.

"Then let's go. By the way, we're walking, if you don't mind."

"The entire time?" she asked with a frown.

"No, just to your place, and then to the donut shop, since I left my Jeep there earlier."

"I can do that," Grace said.

CHAPTER 5

"There. That's much better," Grace said after she came out of her bedroom, now changed into slacks and a nice blouse.

"I know that you have at least *one* pair of blue jeans," I said, "but I rarely see you wear them."

"I'm saving them for a special occasion," she answered with a smile. "Let's go start sleuthing."

"I'm ready if you are," I said. As we walked around the bend of the road from her home to the donut shop, we had to go right past Gabby Williams's gently used clothing shop. None of my clothes would have been suitable candidates for ReNEWed, but I had a hunch that everything of Grace's would be welcomed with open arms. Gabby was gruff and easily offended, but she was also one of the best sources of information in all of April Springs. We didn't even have to drive to her store, since it was just past my shop on the way to the town square. I shivered a little when I thought about that building where I'd found Harley's body, but I suppressed it just as quickly. I knew that I'd probably have trouble sleeping that night, but I wasn't about to let the images haunt my waking hours.

As I walked past Donut Hearts, Grace asked, "Suzanne, are you lost? Your Jeep is parked in back, isn't it?"

"Yes, but we don't have to drive to where I want to go first."

Grace's smile wavered a bit. "We're going to speak with Gabby, aren't we?"

"I thought you two had worked out your differences?" I asked her. In fact, I'd been there to witness it, and if the peace that had been brokered was now gone, I wasn't aware of it.

"No, we're fine. I just don't see any reason to push my luck with her."

"You're kidding, right? I constantly stay in the woman's doghouse, but does that keep me from pressing her for answers when I need them?"

"You're a special case," she said.

"How so?"

"I don't know, but for some reason, Gabby seems to really like you."

"If that's affection, I'd hate to see animosity," I said as I approached her door.

"I can tell you from firsthand experience that it's ugly, that's for sure," Grace answered.

I stopped at the door, ready to turn the handle and go inside, when I noticed a sign displayed prominently in the window. "THE SHOP WILL BE CLOSED ALL DAY TODAY. COME BACK TOMORROW."

I gestured to the glass where it was taped. "I didn't even know she was leaving town."

"I didn't, either. When do you think she'll be back?"

I looked at Grace oddly and then back at the sign again. "Tomorrow," I said as I tapped out the word with my knuckle.

"Sure, but when did she put it up? It's pretty clever, actually. It leaves her free to return whenever she'd like. If it was first posted yesterday, one might assume that she's coming back sometime today, but if it just went up, then we've lost one of our best sources in town for the next twenty-four hours."

"I doubt that you're really all that unhappy about it," I said.

"Don't be so sure. Gabby's useful," Grace said. "I never

denied that. So, if we can't use her as a resource, who do we speak with in her place?"

I was trying to come up with an answer when I heard my name being called from down the street. I looked over to see Christine Hargraves, my friend and Emily's mother, approaching.

"Hi, Christine," I said when she got to us.

"Hello. Hi, Grace." Christine had clothes covered in a dry-cleaning bag in her arms, and when she looked at Gabby's sign, she frowned. "Where could she be?"

"Did you have an appointment with her to resell those things?" I asked her.

"No, but I just assumed that she'd be here. I brought some of my nicer things by a few days ago, but she wouldn't even look at them until I had them dry-cleaned first. Can you imagine that?"

"From Gabby, I have no problem believing it. How are Emily and the guys doing?" The guys in question were her three stuffed animals she'd had since she'd been a little girl. Not only was her business named for them, Two Cows and a Moose, but they were prominently displayed in the newsstand as well. Emily often dressed them up in costumes, and I had to admire her business acumen. A great many folks came by just to see what they were wearing at the moment.

"They're all perfect," she said with a grin. "Have you been by the shop lately?"

"No, not for a while," I admitted. "What are they wearing?"

"She's dressed all three of them up as snowmen! I suppose I should say two snow cows and a snow moose, to be proper. They're so adorable in their costumes. I don't know where she gets her creative streak. It's certainly not from her father or me." She looked at me for a second before she asked, "Were you looking for Gabby, too?"

"I thought I'd take a chance and try her," I said.

"To talk or to shop?" Christine asked us.

"Would both be an answer that suited you?" Grace asked with a grin.

"I know the two of you. You're looking into Harley Boggess's murder together, aren't you?"

I simply shrugged, but as I did, Grace nodded enthusiastically as she replied in the affirmative.

Christine looked pleased. "I thought as much. Actually, I might be able to help you."

"You?" I asked. "I wasn't aware that you even knew Harley."

"In passing, but that's not particularly relevant. I was out taking a stroll alone a few nights ago while my husband was home building one of his model planes, and I happened to spot Harley having an argument under the town clock."

"Who was he arguing with?" Grace and I asked nearly simultaneously.

"Ordinarily I wouldn't say anything, since I detest gossip, but this might be significant, so I'll make an exception this once."

She was clearly reluctant to talk, and I knew that I couldn't compel her to if she didn't want to. Jake and his fellow officers had ways to make people talk to them, but all that Grace and I had were our friendly faces and willing ears. It was enough more times than not, but it didn't always work.

"Don't worry, Christine. We'll keep whatever you tell us in confidence," Grace said.

"If we can," I added.

"I understand," she said as she nodded. "I'm probably just being silly making such a big fuss out of it. It might be easily explained away."

"Then let's do that person the service of allowing them the opportunity," I said gently. "Otherwise, we'll always assume the worst."

"I never thought of it that way," Christine said, and after a few brief nods, she added, "Harley was having a rather testy conversation with Nathaniel Bloom. I doubt that either man even noticed me, but I surely noticed them."

"Did you happen to hear what they were arguing about?" I asked her.

"I couldn't tell, but both men were deadly serious," she replied. "I shouldn't have used that expression, but you know what I mean."

"Was there anything physical about their confrontation?" Grace asked her.

"What do you mean, did anyone throw a punch? Not that I could tell. I just saw them for less than a minute as I crossed the street in front of the newspaper building. Honestly, I was embarrassed for them both, and I didn't want them to know that I was even there."

"Thank you for telling us about it," I said.

"Of course. As I said, I'm sure that it was nothing." She glanced at the sign again, and then she said, "Well, I suppose I should take these things back home until Gabby returns. Good-bye, ladies."

After we said our farewells, Grace asked me, "What do you make of that?"

"It sounds like we need to speak with Nathaniel Bloom," I said as I glanced at my watch. "If we're lucky, he'll still be in his office." Nathaniel not only served on the city council with Harley, but his office was in the same general area just off Viewmont Avenue, the road that led to Union Square. "Let's go see if we can find him," I said as Grace and I turned and headed for my Jeep.

I agreed with her about riding instead of walking. The office was definitely too far to make it on foot if we had any hope of meeting Momma in time.

CHAPTER 6

"**M**R. BLOOM, DO YOU HAVE a second?" I asked after our first suspect answered the door. Nathaniel Bloom was tall, heavyset, and his hair was beginning to fade away into nothingness, no matter how much he tried to disguise the fact. He was wearing an old-fashioned tweed suit, and I half expected him to light a meerschaum pipe. "Grace and I would love to have a word with you."

"Of course," he said as he stepped aside to let us in. He didn't have a secretary or a receptionist, so it was just him. Looking around, I could see that the space was masculine to the extreme, featuring a sea of leather, quarter-sawn oak, and dry-stacked stone everywhere. "Are you two ladies looking to change your investment advisors?" he asked as he sat behind his massive desk. I knew that he handled other people's money for a living, but the implication that I had any worth investing was amusing.

"Sorry, but my net worth is in my checking account, and last month I had to pay a fee for the balance being under the required minimum."

Grace nodded. "Our investments are handled through work. Thanks for offering, though."

He looked puzzled by our statements. "I understand, but I'm not entirely certain what I can do for you."

"Mr. Bloom, you can help us with something far more important than money," I said.

"Please, call me Nathaniel. I find that rather hard to believe," the man said gravely. "Money allows you to do the things in this life you were destined to do."

"I don't need much to be a donut maker," I said.

"And I'm fairly happy myself," Grace added.

"Very well, we've established that you two are in no need of my services, but the question still remains. If not money, then what?"

"We're here to talk about Harley Boggess," I said.

"Yes, that was most unfortunate," Bloom said.

"I'd say it was more than that, especially for Harley," Grace replied.

"I agree. We were colleagues in the battle to keep April Springs vibrant on the city council," he said. "I'll miss working side by side with him for the greater good of our community."

Was this guy answering questions or running for office? "Surely you didn't *always* get along," I said, trying to act as sweet and innocent as I could manage.

"When it counted, in the end, we were fellow servants of the people," he intoned as though he were addressing a joint session of the legislature.

"Even recently?" I asked him.

Bloom looked at us, each in our turn, and then he said slowly, "I'm not sure what you've heard, but whatever it might be, I can assure you both that it isn't true." He glanced at his watch, and then he stood. "Now, if you'll excuse me, I have a client coming in very soon. I've been working on his portfolio all morning, and I really can't delay our meeting, lest he change his mind once more and drive me completely mad."

"We'll leave as soon as he arrives," Grace said. Since neither one of us made any move to leave, Bloom reluctantly settled back into his chair.

"I suppose you're referring to the discussion Harley and I

had the night before last," he said. "I wasn't aware that anyone had witnessed that."

"A small town has big ears," I said.

"Who told you about it?" he asked, trying to sound nonchalant.

"I'd rather not say," I replied. I'd told Christine that I'd keep her name out of our investigation if I could, and I'd meant it. "What were you two arguing about?"

"As a matter of fact, it concerned the acquisition of something that relates to you," he said as he frowned at me.

That was a shocker. "Were you two arguing about trying to buy my donut shop, because if you were, I can save you some grief. It's not for sale."

"No, I'm talking about the empty building on Viewmont Avenue."

"What? The old lawyer's office beside the jail? What has that got to do with me?" I'd glanced over at that building a hundred times on my way back and forth from Union Square, and honestly, it had become a blank spot in my vision over time.

"Don't be coy with me, young lady."

"I only wish that were the case," I said. "Unfortunately, I don't have a clue what you're talking about."

"I find that hard to believe, since the deed is in your name," he said.

"I don't know where you're getting your facts, but you're sadly mistaken," I said. "I own the building that Donut Hearts is in, and the cottage where I live with my husband. That's it."

"Perhaps you should have a talk with your mother," Bloom said, beginning to stand again. "I won't keep you from it, and it sounds as though it's long past due."

"That can wait until later," I said. "We're not finished talking about Harley."

Bloom didn't sit back down this time. Instead, he leaned his considerable bulk on his desk. I was glad it was made of stout oak, or I would have worried that he might bring the entire thing down. "I only have one more minute I can spare," he said.

"Then tell us why you wanted the building," I said, still not wanting to identify it as mine.

"Some of the members of the community were going to try to use it to entice Teresa Logan into serving as our town's attorney," he said. Teresa had been in town less than six months, but it appeared that she'd already made quite an impression, at least on the men of April Springs. I liked her fine myself, other than her propensity to flirt with my husband, something that didn't seem to bother him at all.

"Well, I can't help you there, because I still don't believe that it's mine to sell," I said. "Is that really what you two were arguing about?"

"As I said, there was no argument; it was a friendly discussion, at least at that point."

"What changed?" Grace asked him.

"Amber North's name came up," he admitted with an open scowl.

"Amber? What about her?" Amber ran a cleaning service for businesses that covered three counties, working mostly at night after the staffs had gone home for the day. Now that she had four employees of her own, I'd heard that she didn't do much cleaning anymore herself.

"Harley was seeing her. Didn't you know?"

"Harley? And Amber? Amber North. Are you sure?" Harley had been many things, but reckless wasn't one of them, and dating Amber North could only be described as taking his life into his own hands. She was notorious for her temper with any gentleman unfortunate enough to spawn her ire.

"I don't believe it," Grace said.

"I'm having trouble with it myself," I said.

"If you don't trust my word, ask around. It wasn't as though they were trying to hide their relationship from anyone."

"So why were you two arguing about Amber? Were you seeing her, too?" Grace asked pointedly.

I wasn't expecting the investment man to start laughing at the notion, but that's exactly what he did. After he got himself back under control, he said, "Excuse me, but I'd sooner kiss a porcupine on the lips than date that woman."

"Then why were you fighting over her?"

"She was interfering with Harley's sense of right and wrong," Bloom said. "The woman has never liked me, and since they started seeing each other, Harley became downright confrontational in our council meetings. If you don't believe me, ask the mayor. He bore the brunt of Harley's outbursts more than I ever did."

"We will," I said. Had Bloom not heard about George's absence? He couldn't have. If he'd had the slightest inkling that our mayor was AWOL, I was certain that he would have brought it up. "Where were you this morning between nine and eleven-fifteen?" I asked him, since those were the hours the building opened and when I'd found Harley dead.

"As I told you before, I've been here at my desk the entire time, prepping for my meeting this afternoon," he said. "Why do you ask?"

"It might be helpful to know, that's all," I said. It didn't even occur to him that I'd been asking him for an alibi, as flimsy as it was.

I was about to ask my next question when there was a knock on the door. Seth Lancaster, a good customer of mine at the donut shop, poked his head in. "Is this a bad time? I can wait outside if you'd like."

That was all Bloom needed to get rid of us. "No, you're right on time, Seth. The ladies were just leaving."

"Are you sure?" he asked as he glanced in my direction. "I don't mean to push you out, Suzanne."

"We were on our way out," I said as I stood, putting on my brightest smile. As I offered Bloom my hand, I said, "We'll speak again."

"I'm sure that I've told you everything I know," he said with a forced grin.

"We'll see about that," I said. Grace stood, and after giving Seth a more genuine smile, we left the office.

"Suzanne, did you really not know that you were a land baron?" Grace asked me the moment we were outside.

"It's got to be some kind of mistake," I said.

"It didn't sound like it was to me," she answered. "Maybe you should do what Bloom suggested and ask your mother about it."

"Oh, you can bet I'm going to do exactly that," I said. As we headed over to the Boxcar for our lunch rendezvous with my mother, I resolved that I was going to get some answers and find out if what I'd just heard was actually true or not.

CHAPTER 7

To my surprise, Momma was already at the diner waiting for us. Trish had offered us both a quick hello, but she was swamped with diners waiting to pay, so there wasn't much opportunity for small talk.

"Girls, I've got some news to share with you," Momma said brightly as we sat down at her table.

"Me first," I said abruptly.

She looked startled by my declaration. "Fine. Go on. What's so urgent?"

"I just have one question to ask you, and I need you to tell me the truth. Momma, do I own the empty old building on Viewmont Avenue?"

Her face went ashen, and I knew that what Nathaniel had told me was true. "Oh, dear," was all that she managed to say.

"Seriously? That's the best you can do? What else do I own, Momma?" I gestured around the Boxcar Grill. "Is this place mine, too?"

"Lower your voice, Suzanne. You're attracting entirely too much attention," Momma said, trying to hush me.

I looked around and saw that she was right. Taking a softer tone, I asked, "Why did you buy that building and put it in my name? Was it for taxes, or was there some other, more nefarious reason behind it?"

"The truth of the matter is that I didn't buy it for you," she replied calmly.

"Why don't I give you two some privacy?" Grace asked as she started to stand.

Nearly in unison, Momma and I both said, "Sit down, Grace."

She did as she was told, a rare feat for her, but one I couldn't take the time to acknowledge.

"Please explain yourself," I told my mother, trying to keep my temper in check. I knew that she loved me, and I loved her too, but that woman could push buttons in me that I didn't even know existed. "How has the town not repossessed it for back taxes? I know that *I've* never paid any on it."

"I've been covering the expenses on the building for many years, but they never amounted to much."

"Okay, but if you didn't buy it for me, then who did?"

"Your father."

"What?" I asked her incredulously. "My dad has been dead a long time. When did all of this happen, and why didn't you tell me about it before I found out from a perfect stranger?"

"I wanted to, believe me. I begged and pleaded with your father to let me tell you, but he steadfastly refused, even to the point of binding me to a promise beyond the grave. I was never to mention it unless things got extremely dire for you. I nearly told you after you discovered that Max had cheated on you and that you were leaving him, but then you got a sizable divorce settlement, and you didn't need the money. The only escape clause your father gave me was that if you came to me with the knowledge that the building belonged to you, I was free from my promise to him."

"Why didn't he want me to know about it?" I asked. Though my father had been gone a great many years, rarely a day went by that I didn't think of him at least once, whether it was when I made a donut favorite of his long before I'd ever opened my own shop or saw a red flannel shirt, one of his choicest things to wear, or heard a certain laugh that reminded me of him. None of what I was learning now made any sense to me.

"He was worried that he wouldn't always be there for you," Momma finally said. "No, he didn't have a premonition about his death. Your father was just being pragmatic. He had an opportunity to buy the building, and he decided that it would make a good safety net for you if you ever got into trouble and he wasn't there to help you out of it."

"So it's really mine, free and clear?"

Momma nodded. "It's not worth a fortune, but if you fix it up and rent it out, it might provide you and Jake with a nice little supplemental income. If you don't care to be a landlord, I'll buy it from you myself above the fair market price. It's your decision." She sighed before she spoke again. "To be honest with you, Suzanne, it's a relief that you finally know the truth. I hate keeping secrets from you."

"Are there any more I don't know about?" I asked her, almost afraid to hear what she had to say.

Before she could answer, Trish joined us. "Sorry about the cold greeting, but when folks are clamoring to give me money, I have a hard time resisting." She seemed to notice the expressions on our faces as she added, "Is this a bad time?"

"You're fine, dear," Momma said.

It had saved my mother from answering my question for now, but sometime in the near future, I planned to bring it up again. I hadn't known about the building. What else was she keeping from me?

"Excellent," Trish said. "Are you ladies ready to order?"

"I'll have the special," Momma said with conviction, no doubt happy for the interruption.

"Two," Grace said as she held up two fingers.

"You might as well make it three," I echoed.

"I love it when my life is this easy," Trish said. "Sweet teas, coming right up."

After she was gone, Momma said, "Now, on to my news. I spoke with Curtis Daniels. It was quite illuminating."

I thought about pursuing my last line of questioning, but when I glanced at Grace, she shook her head slightly. Was she reading my mind? Probably not, but we were close, so it wasn't that far a stretch to believe that she knew what I was about to do. Most likely she was right about not pushing my mother any more than I already had, at least not for the moment. After all, she'd just dropped a bombshell on me. It was only fair to give me a little time to come to grips with the information. "What did he have to say?" I asked as Grace nodded in approval.

"It was more about what he wouldn't say," she said. "He brushed me off completely. The man barely shared two words with me before he found a way to get off the phone."

"How exactly is that illuminating?" I asked her, since evidently our definitions of the word varied greatly.

"Suzanne, he's been after some property I own in Union Square for ages. He never fails to bring it up every time that we talk, and yet he didn't even ask me about it when we chatted today."

"So, is that significant?" Grace asked.

"You'd better believe it. I've been keeping him on the hook in order to squeeze more cash out of him, but today, it was as though the deal never even crossed his mind. That's very telling, as far as I'm concerned."

"Remind me never to do business with you, Dot," Grace said with a grin.

"I'd never treat you that way, dear," she said as she reached over and patted my best friend's hand. "You're family, in every way that counts."

"That means a great deal to me," Grace said haltingly. I

glanced over at her and saw that there were tears forming in her eyes. I knew that my mother was a surrogate parent for her, and more importantly, so did Momma. She'd always had a soft spot in her heart for Grace, and sometimes, especially when I'd been a mouthy, rebellious teen, I'd resented it, loudly, but the older I got, the smarter my mother became. It was funny how that worked out.

"How should we approach him?" I asked her as Trish appeared with three glasses of her famous sweet tea.

"Who exactly are we approaching, and can I get in on it?" the grill owner asked me with a laugh.

"Don't you even want to know the circumstances before you volunteer your services?" I asked her, smiling.

"No need. If it's good enough for the three of you, then I'm all in."

"What if we end up going to jail?" Grace asked her.

"Who better to share a cell with than you ladies?"

"Sorry, Trish, but it's nothing quite so dramatic," Momma said, happy to play along.

"Maybe next time, then," the diner's owner said. Was she honestly a little disappointed that we weren't about to do something illegal?

After she was gone, I asked Momma, "Do you have any ideas about how best to approach him?"

"Our best strategy is to just march into his office later today and demand a meeting with him," she said.

"Can't he just refuse to see us?" I asked.

"Not if he still wants that property," Momma said smugly. I had a hunch that she was right, since her instincts were almost always dead on, especially when it came to business. My mother had been the land baron of the family for as long as I could remember, which was what had surprised me even more about my father's purchase. I was upset learning what he'd done, but mostly I was happy to know that he'd been thinking about me and looking out for his baby girl, something I always was to him and would be even now if he were still alive.

"When should we tackle him?" I asked.

"I believe later this afternoon should be just right, since I know he leaves his office promptly at a quarter after four every day, rain or shine. The real question is what should we do in the meantime?"

"If it's okay with you, Grace and I have to go see someone before then," I said.

"Would you care to share the identity of your mystery suspect?" Momma asked.

"It's Amber North," Grace answered softly.

"I don't envy you that visit," Momma said with a slight shudder.

"Do you know her?" I asked my mother. I couldn't imagine the circumstances when those two diverse women would have ever met.

"Our paths have crossed a few times in the past," she said, but when I looked expectantly toward her for more information, none was forthcoming.

"Were you two able to speak with anyone this morning?" Momma asked.

"That's right. We haven't told you about that yet." I recounted our chance encounter with Christine in front of Gabby's shop, keeping her identity a secret, as promised. Chops to Momma. She didn't ask either one of us who our source was. I continued, "After she pointed us in Nathaniel's direction, we went straight to his office. He actually thought we were going to invest with him."

"It's not that ridiculous an idea, Suzanne," Momma said. "Contrary to outward appearances, Nathaniel Bloom does quite well for his clients. A little too well sometimes, if you ask me."

"I'm going to ask you what you mean, if Suzanne won't," Grace said. "Is there something you know that we don't?"

"I'm not saying he's used his position on the city council for the betterment of his financial clients, but some may argue that's the case. Also, he offers better returns than most index funds do, something that is highly suspicious in and of itself."

"Do you have any investments with him?" I asked. Maybe it could serve as a way to get Nathaniel to speak a little more freely with us, and I wasn't above using whatever means I had at my disposal to make that happen.

"No."

When she didn't elaborate, I asked, "Why not?"

Momma frowned before she spoke again. "There's just something about the man that I don't completely trust," she said. "Don't ask me to explain why I feel that way, because it's something I've never been able to quite put my finger on."

"Enough said. I trust your gut," I answered. "We're going to take another run at him, but not right away. I think we'll let him stew overnight before we approach him again."

"So then it's settled," Momma said. "After you and Grace speak with Amber, you and I will tackle Curtis, Suzanne. It sounds like a good strategy to me."

"I just hope we find whoever killed Harley," Grace said.

Trish had approached, loaded down with a full tray, but I'd somehow missed spotting her approach. "I knew you three were up to something," she said triumphantly. "There's no way this much brain power would be gathered together in my simple eatery just to share a meal."

"We thought we might do a little investigating," I admitted, knowing that Trish could be a good source of information, though not as good as Gabby Williams was. "Do you know where Gabby is, by the way?"

"Maybe she and George ran off together," Trish said with a

grin as she placed full plates of roast beef, mashed potatoes and gravy, and peas in front of each of us.

"Don't even kid about that," I said.

"What's this about Gabby and George together?" Momma asked.

Trish took it as an invitation to join us, which I was certain none of us really minded. "They're both missing. Haven't you heard the news?"

I'd neglected to share Gabby's absence with my mother, who looked at me carefully before I got up the nerve to just shrug. "Sorry. I was going to get around to mentioning it."

"I'm sure that you were," Momma said, clearly not certain of that fact at all.

Trish took the opening to say, "I was just kidding about them being together. Gabby is probably off on one of her mysterious overnight trips. I have no idea where our mayor is, but I'm fairly certain that they are miles apart, wherever they are."

"I don't doubt that for a second," Grace said.

Before Momma could ask anything else about Gabby, Trish said, "If you're looking into Harley's murder, you should talk to Megan Gray."

"Megan?" I asked her. "What does she have to do with what happened to Harley?"

"Didn't you know? She's been in love with him for years," Trish said. "The poor woman has been following him around town like some kind of lost puppy dog for years. Haven't you noticed?"

"I suppose I have, now that you mention it. It doesn't make sense, though. If she had a crush on him, why would she kill him?"

Trish smiled as her voice softened. "If she'd left it at a crush, she wouldn't have, but she marched up to him yesterday at that table over there and told him how she felt. I still don't know where she got the nerve to do it."

"How did he react to the news?" I asked her.

"In the worst possible way, if you ask me."

"He rejected her openly?" I asked.

"No, it was worse than that. He laughed at her."

"Wow, she must have been humiliated," Grace said.

"I'd say that was one of her emotions, but there was some fury in her as she left as well," Trish said.

"Isn't she quite a bit younger than Harley?" my mother asked.

"Twenty-five years, at least," Trish said. "Megan's always had daddy issues, so that didn't surprise me. Her father ran off when she was just a kid, and she's been interested in older men just about ever since."

"She's kind of...nondescript, isn't she?" Grace asked.

"Megan's downright mousy," Trish agreed. "But there was nothing submissive about her yesterday."

"Trish, any day would be fine," Jack Jefferson said loudly as he waved his bill at the register up front.

"Hold your horses, Jack," Trish said before she turned to us. "Ladies, if there's any way that I can help, all you have to do is ask. Harley was a bit of a blowhard at times, but he wasn't all bad, and he was always a great tipper. I'll miss him."

Trish got up leisurely and walked to the front, pushing Jack's patience as far as she could without having him explode on the spot.

"Well, what do you think about that?" Grace asked. "Who would have thought that was even possible?"

"It adds another suspect to our list," Momma said. "Suzanne, may I go with you when you interview Megan? I know her mother quite well, so that might be of some assistance, and besides, Grace already has two suspects, and I have only one."

"Grace, what do you think?" I asked her after taking a bite of the delicious lunch.

"It's fine with me. I'm drowning in paperwork, so it will give me a chance to catch up at home while you two are off sleuthing."

Momma reached across the table and patted her hand. "You truly don't mind?"

"Truly," Grace said.

After we finished eating, Grace and I both reached for the bill simultaneously, but Momma was quicker.

"You don't have to treat us to lunch," I told her.

"Nonsense. How often do I get the opportunity to buy lunch for my two favorite women in the world?"

"Don't rob that from her, Suzanne," Grace said with a grin before turning to Momma. "It's nice to be in the top two, but out of curiosity, which one of us is number one?"

"Don't answer that," I said, half in jest but still afraid of what her answer might be.

Once we were outside, Momma said, "I'll be at my place when you're ready for me, Suzanne."

"I'll see you then," I said.

After she was gone, I turned to Grace. "You really don't mind this new arrangement?"

"Not a chance. Talk about classing our group up, your mother puts us over the top. Besides, I know that you'll keep me in the loop." She looked at me intently before she asked, "You will keep me in the loop, won't you?"

"You can count on it," I said. "Are you ready to tackle Amber?"

"I guess that I'm as ready as I'll ever be," Grace said, and we went off in search of the cleaning service owner to see if she could shed any light on what had happened to Harley Boggess.

CHAPTER 8

"**D**O YOU HAVE A SECOND, Amber?" I asked, knocking on her front door repeatedly before she finally answered. "Grace and I would love a few minutes of your time."

"Why? What do you want? Do you have something you need cleaned?"

I didn't have an answer for her, but Grace saved me. "As a matter of fact, Suzanne just learned that she's inherited the old lawyer's building on Viewmont Avenue, and she needs it cleaned from top to bottom. We were wondering if you'd like to bid on the job."

"I don't do bids," Amber said flatly. She had no doubt been cute as a button when she'd been younger, full of curves and no hard edges, but over the years, her cuteness had faded as her weight had increased. It was hard to imagine her with Harley, but then again, I was almost always amazed when any two people managed to find each other. I would have never put my ex-husband Max with my friend Emily either, but that was working out splendidly for both of them, so who was I to judge?

"How do you get new jobs if you don't bid on them, then?" Grace asked her.

"I have a flat rate I charge per hour, and most folks seem happy enough with my system."

"And those that don't?" Grace pushed.

"Then they can go someplace else. It doesn't matter to me

either way. I have enough work to keep everybody on my staff busy. In fact, I'm always on the lookout for more employees." She looked at me intently for a moment, and then she asked, "When should we get started, Suzanne? I might be able to pencil you in for sometime next week, but I'm not making any promises."

"You haven't even told me your rate yet," I reminded her. After she quoted an hourly rate to me, I tried my best not to frown. It was quite a bit more than I would have been willing to pay, even if I were in the market to have someone else do it for me. I wasn't afraid of hard work or getting dirty, either, so when it came time to clean the place up to see what I had, I was sure that I'd be able to do it myself, and if it was too overwhelming, I had enough family and friends who would pitch in without having to be asked twice. I took that fact for granted, something that was actually quite nice. "Let me think about it," I said.

"Sure, but don't wait too long. My schedule fills up pretty fast."

Amber started to close the door on us, but I managed to grab it before she could shut it all of the way. "There's something else that we'd like to discuss with you since we're already here."

"Now?" she asked as she glanced back inside.

"Why, is this a bad time?" Grace asked as we both tried to see if anyone else was there. "You don't have company, do you?"

"No, it's nothing like that. It's just that one of my favorite shows is coming on in ten minutes, and I never miss it."

"We won't overstay our welcome. I promise," I said as I pressed her closer. Grace moved in as well, and if Amber was going to be able to take another breath, she had no choice but to back up into her foyer and allow us to come inside. She obviously didn't want to do that, but finally, she relented and stepped aside.

"Do either one of you want some tap water?" she offered lamely. "Sorry, but it's all that I've got."

I doubted that was true, but we weren't there for the refreshments. "No thanks. We just need a minute of your time, and then we'll be on our way. We understand that you were dating Harley when he died."

"Who told you that? Never mind, I already know. It's not like it was any big secret or anything, but we weren't ready to announce it to the entire world, you know? I bet it was Nathaniel Bloom; he must have shot his mouth off about it. Yeah, Harley and I were dating."

"Did you love him?" Grace asked softly.

"Love? I don't even know what that word means anymore. Maybe. We liked each other's company. Is that love? Who knows? I'm upset somebody killed him, so yeah, maybe I did love him, in my own way."

I hoped if Jake were alive when I died, he'd be more emphatic about how he felt about me. It wasn't very heartwarming. "I'm sorry for your loss," I said automatically. I had too many Southern manners bred into me not to say it, even if I wasn't entirely sure that it was appropriate. "Since you cared so much for him, I'm sure you want to help us find his killer."

Amber pursed her lips. "You two are digging into it, are you? It figures."

"Why do you say that?" Grace asked.

"You're kidding, right? You two have a reputation for being busybodies, if you don't mind me saying so."

"Mind? Why should we mind?" Grace asked, and I could hear her gearing up for a reply that I knew Amber wasn't going to appreciate very much.

Before she could go any further, I said, "Then you understand. Have you two been fighting lately?"

"No, we hardly ever fought at all. The only time we ever really argued was when I thought he was letting other people push him around. I couldn't tolerate that, so I made him see that he needed to stand up for himself more, with George and Nathaniel and Curtis, every last one of them."

So, she wanted him to be more assertive, just not with her. "How did they react to his change of attitude?"

"They didn't like it, but then why should they? Harley was going places, you know? For starters, he was going to run for mayor. That's probably why George stuck that letter opener into his chest."

"Do you honestly believe that George Morris killed him?" I asked.

"Who else could have done it? George had the most to lose, and everybody knows what a hothead he is."

I was about to lose my temper when I took a few deep breaths and got it back under control. If I was anything, it was fiercely loyal to my friends, and George was within my closest inner circle. "Let's assume for a second that George didn't do it. Who else would make your list?"

She frowned for a moment before she answered. "Like I said, lately he didn't get along too well with Nathaniel or Curtis, either."

"We're already looking into both men," I said. "Is there anyone else you can think of?"

"Not off the top of my head," she said. "Now, you two really do need to excuse me. It's about that time."

Hadn't the woman ever heard of a DVR or Tivoing something? I was about to keep her a little longer when Grace surprised me. "What about Megan Gray?"

"What about her?" Amber looked clearly distracted by the approaching show's start.

"She told Harley she loved him," Grace said calmly.

Amber looked at Grace to see if she was kidding, and when she didn't smile in return, Amber shook her head. "That's why she *wouldn't* have killed him."

"How can you be so sure?" I asked her.

"If I ended up dead, sure, she'd be at the head of the list, but she worshipped Harley. As a matter of fact, we both used to laugh about it."

I thought quite a bit less of Harley at the moment, but I couldn't let that stop me from trying to find his killer. "He openly rejected her, though. Doesn't that count for something?"

"You tell me; you're the detectives. I've really got to go. Bye."

"One last thing," I said, stalling her as long as I could manage. "Where have you been all day?"

"I've been right here."

"Can you prove that?" I asked her.

"All day? No, and I don't have to."

"Was anyone here with you at any time?" I asked her.

"I had a few girls here to try out for jobs this morning, but they were all gone by nine thirty." That gave her plenty of time to go to City Hall, kill Harley, and make it back without anyone noticing her absence. "Now go." She used her bulk and forced us out the door before either one of us could say another word.

"That was interesting," Grace said.

"Which part of it?" I asked as we walked back to my Jeep.

"All of it. Amber didn't seem too torn up about Harley's murder, did she?"

"Maybe she's just good at hiding it. Then again, she might not have loved him at all, given her description of how she felt about him."

"Or maybe, just maybe, she's better at it than we're giving her credit for. What if she killed him out of jealousy, and now she's trying to act as though it didn't matter to her one way or the other?"

"It's something we need to keep in mind," I said. "I wonder what show she's hooked on?"

"I'm not sure that I even want to know the answer to that,"

Grace said as I started the engine. "Why don't you drive me home so you can pick up your momma? I expect a full report as soon as you're finished."

"How about if I swing by your place on my way home after we're done?" I offered.

"That sounds great," she said.

After I dropped Grace off at home, I headed over to Momma's place. It was time to start the second phase of the investigation.

I wasn't sure how I was going to balance the involvement between both women, but I'd come up with something. After all, Momma had been right. She hadn't been the only one dining with her two favorite women in the world, and it was up to me to keep them both happy about our arrangements.

CHAPTER 9

"**I**s Momma ready to go?" I asked Phillip as he answered the door. When they'd first gotten married, Momma had left the cottage we'd shared to start her new life, but she'd chosen a home to move into that felt as though she'd lived there forever. There was a warm comfort to the place that suited her, and I admired her ability to move into a new house and make it feel like home so quickly. The only place in the world I felt that was at the cottage I shared with Jake, and I knew that if I ever had to leave it, for what reason I couldn't imagine, I'd never find another place that suited me so perfectly.

"She's on an important call, but she asked me to tell you that she'd be right with you," Phillip said as he stood aside and let me in. The former chief of police had happily settled into retirement, but he hadn't been idle since he'd left the April Springs police department. His latest hobby was researching the history of the town, and usually he could be found poring over old newspapers and journals from long ago. "Make yourself at home," he said.

I looked at their expansive kitchen table and saw that it was currently littered with layer upon layer of all kinds of old papers. "What are you up to?"

"I'm digging into a murder," he said with a grin. "It's taken me quite some time to gather enough information together, but I've finally cracked the case and put all of the pieces of the puzzle together once and for all."

The news surprised me. "Are you talking about Harley Boggess's murder?" I hadn't even realized that he'd been working on the case.

"Oh, no. This all happened eighty years ago," he said excitedly as he led me over to his research. "At the time, they called them all accidents, but I'm positive that at least once, and probably three times, it was homicide."

"How can you be so sure if it all happened so long ago?" I asked, caught up in his enthusiasm. Since Phillip Martin had left the force, our relationship had slowly warmed up to the point where I actually enjoyed being around him.

"Eighty years ago, a man named Copernicus Jones had a wife in April Springs called Faith that died in the bathtub," he said as he pointed to a brief headline in a faded newspaper. "She'd been sick for some time, at least according to Copernicus, and the local doctor wrote it up as an accidental drowning. At the time, nobody seemed to think that it was anything other than what it appeared to be."

"Isn't it possible that it *was* an accident?" I asked.

"Sure, but when it gets complicated is when I started tracing Copernicus's life before he came to April Springs. Three years before he married Faith, he had been married to a woman named Amity he'd met in Union Square. She, too, died in the bathtub. Kind of an odd coincidence, wouldn't you say?"

"I don't believe in coincidences any more than you do," I said. "What was his story with her?"

"He claimed to be out of town, but he was a hard horse-ride away, yet no one saw him that day. Amity's best friend found her, and Copernicus claimed to be so grieved over the loss that he sold everything, including all of Amity's jewelry that she'd inherited from her mother. Apparently it was worth quite a fortune back then."

"Was Faith wealthy as well?" I asked, peering down at the pile that was suddenly beginning to make sense.

"She was indeed," he said with a grin. "Copernicus made even more off her death. But that's not the kicker."

"What was?" I asked, caught up despite myself. Phillip's enthusiasm was catching.

"There was a third wife after Faith that he married in Hudson Creek," he said. "Her name was Harriet."

"Don't tell me. She died in the bathtub, too."

"You'd think so, wouldn't you? But the truth is even stranger than that."

At that moment, Momma came out from the other room. "Suzanne, I'm ready if you are."

"Hang on a second. Phillip's not finished telling me about his investigation."

Momma laughed. "He's caught you up in it too, has he?"

"Dorothea, you can't deny that it's fascinating."

She kissed his cheek fondly. "I wouldn't dream of it. Where are you in the narrative?"

"He just told me about Copernicus's third wife."

"Oh, we're getting to the good part. Don't let me interrupt." Momma was clearly pleased that her husband and I were getting along, but then again, so was I.

"What happened to Harriet?" I asked him.

"She lived to the ripe old age of sixty-three," he said, "and died in her sleep."

I couldn't help but feel let down by the ending of his story. "That's it?"

Phillip grinned at me. "Now ask me about Copernicus."

"What happened to him? I'm guessing that he managed to escape justice for the two murders. Did the police finally figure it out, or did he get away with them?"

"I wouldn't say that he got away with them, exactly," Phillip said.

"Dear, don't keep the poor girl in suspense. Tell her what happened," Momma said.

"I was just getting to it," Phillip said, and then he turned back to me. "Copernicus had an accident of his own. He fell down a flight of stairs and broke his neck not long after he married Harriet."

"Do you honestly believe that *she* killed *him* instead?"

"What do you think? I just uncovered the last piece of evidence that I've been missing. When the police arrived on the scene, the chief noted in his journal that the crime scene looked odd to him from the start, but he could never prove that anything was amiss, so he didn't pursue it."

"What did he find that struck him as so unusual?"

"Harriet's hair was wet, her clothes were damp, and Copernicus's shirt sleeves were both soaked with water."

I thought about it for a moment, and then I said, "Copernicus tried to kill Harriet in the tub, too, but she was too strong for him. She fought back and somehow managed to break his neck. After that, to cover up what she'd done, she shoved his body down the stairs to make it look like an accident."

Phillip smiled as he nodded at me. "That's exactly what I believe happened. I just dug up the chief's journal, and I stumbled across the entry this morning."

"It's a marvelous job of detection," Momma said, "but I'm not sure what good it does anyone. Who are you going to tell, Harriet's great-grandchildren?"

"Dorothea, I don't need to tell anyone. Just uncovering it all is enough for me." He looked at me for approval, and I patted his shoulder. In this case, I agreed with him over my mother, something that I'd sooner die than ever admit.

"Thanks, Phillip. That was fascinating."

"You're welcome. Thank you for listening."

"Now that you've cracked this one, what's next on your agenda?"

"There's a suspicious accident at the sawmill in Maple Hollow that I'm going to investigate. One of the workers was killed 'accidentally,' and three months later, the mill operator married his widowed wife."

"It could have been a legitimate accident," Momma said.

"I know, but what fun would that be?" he asked with a grin as he began gathering up his papers.

Once we were outside, Momma said, "Sometimes I wonder about my husband's choice of retirement interests."

"I think it's perfect for a former cop," I said. "He gets to solve crimes with no real stakes involved, since the guilty parties are long dead."

"You two seem to be getting along better these days," she said with a smile.

"What can I say? He's growing on me." I didn't want to have that particular discussion, so I asked instead, "Are you ready to tackle Megan?"

"I am, though I'm going to feel a bit like a bully dealing with her. She's quite the mouse, isn't she?"

"Maybe not all of the time," I said. "If we treat her gently, we'll be fine, but don't forget, just because she seems like a victim doesn't mean that she's not a killer, too. Underestimating her capacity for violence could cost us both our lives."

"I understand," Momma said. "Do you have any idea where we might find her?"

"She's bound to be at work at this time of day," I said.

"Where does she work?" Momma asked. "And how do you know that?"

"She gets donuts for her boss sometimes," I explained as we drove to the hospital.

"I thought we were going to her office?" Momma asked me when she realized where we were headed.

"We are. She works in the admitting department."

"Will she be free to speak with us? I'd hate to get her in trouble with her boss."

"Megan told me recently that she works by herself most of the time, so we should be fine." We parked near the administration area, and I found Megan's small office without much trouble. She was with someone at the moment, and the door was closed.

"Should we come back later?" Momma asked me.

"No, let's wait a bit and see how long she'll be." We settled into some chairs outside her space, and I picked up a magazine that was at least ten years old. Momma chose not to read. Instead, I found her staring at me when I looked up. "Is there something I can do for you?"

"Suzanne, how can you be so calm when we're about to interview a potential killer?"

"I don't know," I said as I leafed through the pages, hoping to find something interesting. "Maybe I talk to suspects so often that it's become a bit routine for me."

"Oh, I hope not."

"Why's that?" I asked her.

"The moment you let your guard down, that's when danger is most likely to strike."

I put the magazine back on the pile. "Momma, I don't need to be worried about anything at the moment, or even be particularly cautious, unless you're going to pull a knife on me," I said with a grin. "When we get inside Megan's office, that's when I'll start being careful."

"And in the meantime?"

"We sit and wait," I said.

It wasn't that long after all. Less than ten minutes after we'd arrived, Megan's door opened and the man she'd been speaking with came out with a sheaf of papers, a plastic band on his wrist, and a bewildered look on his face. Whatever he was in for, I didn't envy him.

"Hi, Suzanne," Megan said when she saw me. She looked at me warily, as though my visit had an ulterior motive, which it did. "You can both come on in."

"Megan, this is my mother, Dorothea," I explained as Momma and I entered her small cubicle of an office. I saw that Megan had done what she could to make the paste-tinted walls homier. There were several framed book covers, all featuring masculine men in various stages of undress. As I studied them a little closer, I realized that they all had something else in common, as well. Each and every man depicted on the covers had graying hair, though their bodies were quite a bit younger.

Megan noticed the way I was studying her posters, and she must have misinterpreted it. "I just love to read. Don't you?"

"We do, but Momma and I mostly stick to mysteries," I said as we took our seats across from her desk.

"Oh, I enjoy some mysteries too, mostly cozies, but what I really love is a good romance." She tapped a few keys on her computer, and then she turned to Momma. "Now, how may I help? What procedure are you undergoing, and who is your primary care physician?"

Momma looked startled by the question. "Pardon me?"

"I just assumed that since Suzanne brought you that you were the one checking in," she said.

"Megan, neither one of us is here to be admitted," I said.

She looked puzzled by my statement. "Then why are you in the admitting office?"

"We came to talk to you about Harley Boggess," I said.

I'd been watching her closely, but my focus wasn't all that necessary. Megan's reaction was clear and immediate. "Why? Have you heard something about who killed him?"

"No, not yet," I said.

Before I could say another word, she blurted out, "Suzanne, you're the one who found him. How bad was it?"

"It wasn't pleasant," I said.

"Did he look tortured, or was he peaceful?"

How was I supposed to answer a question like that? I thought about it for a moment before I spoke. "He looked as though he were taking a nap." In spite of the letter opener sticking in his chest, I wisely failed to add.

"I can't believe he's really gone."

"You two had a relationship, didn't you? I'm sorry for your loss."

Megan blushed a bit. "It wasn't a relationship. It's no secret that I was in love with him, but he didn't feel the same way about me."

Momma said softly, "That must have been terrible for you, dear."

"You'd think so, wouldn't you?" Megan asked. "I was mooning after the man for years, and when I finally got the nerve up to tell him how I felt, he laughed in my face."

"How humiliating," I said. "How did that make you feel?"

"The truth? Certainly I was upset for a bit, but the more I thought about it, the more I realized that he'd done me a favor. I knew then and there that I needed to change."

"How so?" Momma asked in that voice that made folks want to confess everything to her. I didn't know how she managed the inflection, but I would have loved to learn how she did it.

"It all goes back to the fact that my father left my mother on my thirteenth birthday," she said after biting her lower lip. "He just disappeared, and ever since, I've been trying to get an older man's approval. I know it sounds ridiculous, but I didn't even know that I'd been doing it until Harley pointed it out to me. Was it cruel the way he reacted? Probably, but it was the shock I needed. I wish he were still here, so I could thank him for waking me up. I know that no matter how hard I try, I'll never get my father's admiration, either in reality or through a surrogate."

"Is the therapy helping?" Momma asked softly, and Megan's jaw dropped for a moment.

"How did you know?"

"You just sound as though you've had a little help dealing with the issue," Momma assured her.

"Yes, we get three free psych consults a year, so I thought I'd take advantage of our insurance. Dr. Jefferson is amazing! In less than an hour, he rooted out the heart of my problems, and with his help, I'm going to overcome them. I just know it!"

It appeared that Megan had shifted her focus from Harley to her new shrink with relative ease. This woman clearly needed romance in her life, even if it was just in her own mind. I knew plenty of women who adored romance novels and led perfectly normal, happily married or single lives. I just couldn't be sure that Megan was necessarily one of them. "When was the last time you saw Harley?" I asked her.

"When he rejected me," she admitted.

"And not after?" Momma asked.

"No, that was it. The last time I saw him, he was laughing at me."

"Megan, if you don't mind us asking, where were you this morning? Have you been at work all day?" I asked.

"Yes, I've been here at my desk since I punched in. Why do you ask?"

I ignored her question. "You start at nine, don't you?"

"Yes, and I work until five, with thirty minutes for lunch. I always spend it here, reading." Even though mysteries weren't her forte, she finally got it. "Suzanne, you're asking me for an alibi, aren't you?"

I could have denied it, but why bother? "I don't have much choice. Some folks overheard your exchange with Harley," I said. "Naturally you'd be a suspect."

"Are you both working for the police now?" she asked, raising her voice as she looked from Momma to me.

"No, but we're often in close consultation with them," I replied, which was true enough. I consulted with my husband on a daily basis, from what we'd have for dinner to the movie we might watch afterward. That might not have been what she meant, but I couldn't help that, could I?

"Like I said, I've been here all day," she said.

"With no breaks?" I asked her.

"I have one at ten thirty every morning, but it's only ten minutes, so I didn't have time to go from here to City Hall, kill Harley, and make it back on time." She looked down at her desk to compose herself, and then she added, "Now if you'll excuse me, I have a client coming in three minutes, and I need to print out some paperwork before she arrives."

I touched Momma's arm, and we stood. "Thanks for your time."

Megan didn't even respond.

Once we were outside of the hospital, Momma said, "It appears that Megan has a solid alibi for the time of the murder."

"Do you think so? I was actually thinking that her story means that she's still a viable suspect," I replied.

"How so? She said she was here the entire time."

"Momma, we can't just take her word for it. How can we know how long her break really was? No one is around her office to see when she comes and goes, so we don't know. For all we know, she could have been gone for half an hour, which would have been plenty of time to find Harley, kill him, and then get back here before anyone even realized that she was even gone."

Momma frowned. "If that's the case, then how can we possibly find the truth?"

"I'll call Jake and tell him what we just learned. He can pull the hospital's security video and see if Megan's story holds water."

"Does he often do what you ask him to, I mean in his official capacity?"

"Not necessarily, but when it comes to his investigations, he's not too proud to take help from anyone who can help him catch a killer."

"This is all rather more difficult than it seems, isn't it?" she asked me.

"It takes a certain mindset, that's all."

"You don't give yourself enough credit, Suzanne."

"Maybe not. I just do the best I can, stumbling along until I find the one clue that leads me to the truth."

"It's a great deal more complicated than that, and we both know it." Momma glanced at her watch. "We've got some time to kill before we speak with Curtis Daniels. What should we do in the meantime?"

"Let's go over there anyway and see if we can catch him by surprise."

"Is that wise?" she asked me.

"Who knows? All I know is that the quicker we figure out what really happened to Harley, the better I'll sleep at night."

"Then by all means, let's go."

CHAPTER 10

"Dot, what are you doing here?" Curtis Daniels asked as Momma and I walked into his outer office. He was at his secretary's desk taking her to task over something she'd done, and the man was clearly upset about whatever it was. "I'll be with you in a second," he said. "Wendy, this is simply unacceptable. Do you understand?"

"Yes, sir," his secretary said as she rubbed her hands raw from the stress of being upbraided. She was clearly not happy about the scolding, especially in front of us.

For some reason that satisfied Curtis, and as he turned to us, he said, "I told you earlier, I don't have anything to say to you."

"I think you'll want to hear this, Curtis," Momma said brusquely.

"I don't know if you've heard or not, but I just lost my partner. I don't have time for your games today. Now if you'll excuse me, I have work to do."

"Very well," Momma said. "If that's your attitude, I'm donating the land you've been after to the Natural Conservancy Brotherhood this afternoon. I could use the tax write-off more than what you've been willing to pay me for it, and as you said, you have enough to deal with right now without me meddling in your business."

"Hang on. Don't be so hasty. I'm sure that I can carve out a few minutes for you."

"Mr. Daniels, you asked me to remind you that you have

a meeting with the Charlotte attorneys in ten minutes," the secretary reminded him.

"This won't take long," he said. "Hello, Suzanne. If you'd like to wait out here, I'm sure that Wendy would be happy to get you something to drink."

"Actually, I thought I'd tag along with Momma," I said as I smiled.

He looked uncertainly at my mother, who nodded her approval. Seeing that he wasn't going to win that battle, Curtis immediately became the gracious host. "Of course. Let's go into my office."

Once we were inside and the door was closed, Curtis sat behind his massive desk and faced us. "Now, what's this nonsense about donating that land? It's much too valuable to give it to the tree huggers, Dot, and you know it."

"I happen to like their cause," Momma said.

"Then why are you here?" he asked her pointedly. Evidently the gloves were now off.

"I may still be interested in selling the land to you, but it's conditional."

"Upon what?" he asked her, never giving me a second look. I didn't blame him. Momma was clearly in charge of this meeting, no matter what the topic might be.

"You have to answer a few questions for us before I'll even consider your offer," she said.

Curtis pushed away from his desk and leaned back in his chair. "It can't be that easy. I don't get it. What's the catch?"

"Only that you answer truthfully, fully, and to the best of your ability," Momma said.

"It sounds as though you're asking me to testify," Curtis said with a partial smile.

"Take it as you will. I need your word, Curtis."

"Fine. If it's that important to you, I'll answer you if I can."

"Where were you in your progress to dissolve the company when Harley was murdered?"

Curtis didn't answer immediately, and I wondered if we were going to get a true answer, no matter what he'd just promised my mother. "We were in the final stages," he admitted. "We were just waiting for the final audit so I'd know what it was costing me to buy him out. I suppose it's no big secret that we weren't happy with each other anymore. That blasted woman started getting into his head, and she was slowly ruining him, if you ask me."

"Are you referring to Amber North?" I asked him. So much for me being the silent witness to the proceedings.

"Yes, of course. Who else? She thought I was taking advantage of Harley, when in truth, I was bending over backwards to make our partnership work."

I doubted the veracity of what he was saying, but he was convincing nonetheless. I knew my mother could hold her own doing business with him, but I also realized that he would have eaten me alive if I'd come there alone.

"What happens now?" she asked softly.

"Who knows? That's why the attorneys are coming in. They're going to help me straighten this mess out."

"Did you have a surviving partnership clause in your contract, by any chance?" Momma asked him.

"It's a great deal more complicated than that, Dot."

"Answer the question, Curtis," Momma said icily.

"Yes and no," he finally admitted.

"Meaning?"

"Meaning it's not that easy to explain. There were riders and conditions that I can't remember, thus the attorney visit."

"But ultimately, you gain control of the company, and probably Harley's share of the business as well."

"Don't you think I know that I have to be a suspect in his

murder?" Curtis asked as he stood and began pacing behind his desk. "Your husband has already been to see me," he added as he pointed to me.

"You can't blame him. He's just doing his job," I said. "Did you happen to provide him with an alibi when you spoke?"

"Ask him yourself," Curtis snapped at me.

Momma frowned. "I thought you were going to cooperate."

He shrugged, and after a moment, he said, "I happened to be in Union Square all morning looking at some of our holdings."

"Why were you doing that?" Momma asked him.

"We were going to have to liquidate several properties we owned jointly in order to pay Harley for his half of the business."

"Something you are no longer required to do," Momma said.

"Don't read too much into it, Dot."

"Can anyone verify you were there?" I asked him.

"No one was with me the entire time, if that's what you're asking me. Right now I feel as though I can't turn around without someone taking note of it, but I have a question for you two. You're both friends with the mayor, who happened to work in the office where Harley's body was found. Why isn't anyone asking him these questions?"

I wasn't about to tell him that George was missing.

That didn't stop Momma, though. "As soon as he is found, I'm certain that he'll have a reasonable explanation."

I wanted to cover my head in my hands. Momma had just revealed something that might end up being extremely incriminating about George, and what was worse, she'd told it to one of our main suspects.

"He's missing? And you're here grilling me? Why would he run, Dot, if he didn't have anything to do with Harley's murder, which just happened to take place in his chair at his desk in his office with his letter opener?"

"He'll be duly questioned soon enough," Momma said, "but right now, we're here speaking with you."

Curtis frowned a moment before he spoke again. "You know what? I don't want that land after all. By the time I'm free to buy it when the legalities of this mess are all straightened out, you'll have disposed of it anyway, so go ahead and donate it to the tree-huggers for all I care. Now if you'll excuse me, I have a meeting with the attorneys to prepare for."

The dismissal was clear.

Momma and I did the only thing that we could do; we stood up and left.

My mother waited out on the sidewalk before she said, "Suzanne, I can't believe that I just did that. I didn't think. I just blurted out the fact that George was missing, and it shifted the focus of the entire conversation away from where we wanted it to be. I'm so sorry."

"It happens," I said, trying to stay calm about her lapse in judgment.

"Not to me, it doesn't. Can you ever forgive me?"

"Don't worry about it, Momma. Curtis was bound to find out sooner or later."

"Perhaps, but I had no right to be the one who told him."

"Let's not worry about that right now, Momma," I said as we made our way to my Jeep. Ordinarily she refused to ride in it on principle, but since this was my investigation, I hadn't given her a choice. "Do you mind if I take you home now?" Before she could voice her regrets again, I added, "It's got nothing to do with what happened in there. I just need to catch up with Grace and tell her what we discovered."

"And recount my error to her as well, no doubt."

"It's part of it, Momma, but don't be too hard on yourself. Grace and I have slipped up plenty in the past ourselves."

"Honestly?" Momma asked me hopefully.

"You have no idea. I'd tell you, but I couldn't stand the embarrassment."

"That makes me feel somewhat better," she said.

"Why wouldn't it?" I asked her with a grin. "In the end, we're all just amateurs doing our best to track down killers. As a whole, I think we do a pretty good job of it."

"So then, does that mean that you're not firing me?" she asked me timidly as I dropped her off at her front door.

"No, you get two more strikes before that happens," I answered. I hadn't wanted the news of George's absence to get out, but I knew that sooner or later, the entire town of April Springs would find out that he was gone. It was really just a matter of bad timing more than anything else, and I wasn't about to chastise my mother about it. Why would I? She was doing a pretty good job of that herself.

Once she was inside, I headed the Jeep toward Grace's house.

It was time to tell her what we'd learned, no matter how little it felt like at the moment.

CHAPTER 11

"COME ON INSIDE, SUZANNE. IT'S freezing out here," Grace said as she greeted me at her front door. I didn't think it was all that cold, but then again, Grace had a tendency to be warm blooded at times. "Did you have any luck with your interviews?"

"A little," I said, and then I brought her up to speed on what Momma and I had learned.

"So," she said after I finished, "we now have alibis for all of our suspects, as sketchy as they are. One of them has to be lying to us."

"At least one, but that's not the only possibility," I said.

"I'm listening."

"We may not have even found the real killer yet."

"Do you think there's another suspect somewhere out there?" Grace asked me as she took my jacket and hung it up by the door.

"If there is, we'll have to keep our eyes and ears open. I've been trying to call George on his cellphone all day, but it goes straight to voicemail. Where could he have gone?"

"I don't see any possible way that he killed Harley, no matter how much of a pain the man was to him."

"I don't either, Grace," I said hastily. "But that doesn't mean that I wouldn't like to hear what he has to say about what happened in his office today. With Gabby gone too, it's kind of a troubling trend."

"That's one mystery solved, at least. She's back in town," Grace said with a smile.

"What? How do you know that?"

"I got bored waiting around here for you, so I decided to take a walk through the park to clear my head. I figured maybe I'd get some insights into our investigation, and the worst-case scenario was that I got a little exercise. While I was out, I decided to stroll over to Gabby's, and I got there just as she was taking the sign off her door."

"Where had she been?" I asked. I'd driven right past ReNEWed on my way to Grace's, but I must have been so preoccupied with the investigation that I hadn't even noticed the sign announcing Gabby's absence was gone. Some detective I was turning out to be.

"She said that she decided on the spur of the moment to close the shop and take a drive," Grace said. "At least that's what she told me. Suzanne, she was shocked when I told her that Harley had been murdered in George's office this morning. There's no way she could have faked that reaction."

"We never really considered her a suspect, so it's not all that surprising," I said.

"With Gabby, I figured that we couldn't rule her out, even if she didn't have a connection with Harley. Her first response to the news was a little troubling, though."

"How did she react?"

"Before I even told her that George was missing, she asked how he was taking the news."

I thought about it a moment before I spoke. "That's not that odd. After all, the man's office is a crime scene. That's enough to upset anyone."

"Sure it is, but then she added, 'This isn't going to look good for him,' and that's before I even said anything about him taking off."

"Why does everyone keep sharing that news?" I asked, a little peeved that Grace had repeated something we were trying to keep under wraps, just as Momma had done earlier.

"Hey, don't bite my head off," Grace said as she held her palms up in a motion to calm me down. "I figured that for most folks in town, it was already common knowledge."

"I'm sorry," I said. "Momma told Curtis, and now you've said something to Gabby. I'm afraid that George is going to be tried and convicted by the public before he even gets a chance to explain himself."

"I get that, but you have to admit that it's an awfully big coincidence to swallow," Grace said. "There's no denying it, any way you look at it. Taking off around the time his main rival was murdered in the man's own office has all kinds of red flags waving."

"I don't like the way it looks any more than you do, but just this once, we're going to work with the assumption that the two facts are totally unrelated."

"If you say so, boss. After all, I'm just the hired hand around here," Grace said with a smile.

"You're more than that, and we both know it. What should we do next? I'm afraid we've exhausted the questions we can ask our suspects, and short of taking a poll door to door, I don't know how to stir up any more suspects at the moment."

"I wish we could get inside Harley's office and have a look around," Grace said. "How hard would it be to do it without Curtis noticing?"

"Between him and his secretary, I'd say that it was pretty much impossible."

"How about his house, then?" Grace suggested.

"Probably just as tough, but we can't go there until Jake is finished with it. Even then, he's probably not going to appreciate us nosing around behind him."

"Is there the slightest chance that our investigation bothers him more than he's letting on?" she asked me.

"Probably, but as long as we don't try to beat him to the killer, we should be fine," I said.

"That doesn't leave us with much that we can do, does it?"

"We'll just have to find a way to make do within our limitations. I'm not about to cross Jake without having a very good reason."

"I don't blame you a bit," Grace said. "Listen, if there's nothing else we can do at the moment, I've got a few things still on my desk that need to be handled. Do you mind?"

I glanced at my watch and saw that it was nearly time for Jake to come home. I knew if he got there first, he'd thaw a batch of the chili he loved to make, and I didn't think my stomach could take another meal of it so soon. My only hope was to beat him home and cook something for us myself. "No, that works out fine with me. What does your day look like tomorrow?"

"If I can get through this paperwork, I'll be able to take off right about when you're closing the donut shop for the day."

"Let's meet up then and see if either one of us has been able to come up with something else to do that won't burn too many bridges," I suggested.

"Good luck with that. I'll see you tomorrow," she said as I left her place.

Jake wasn't home yet, and I didn't really feel like cooking something from scratch. I pulled a frozen lasagna that I'd made a few weeks earlier from the freezer, being careful to avoid any skin contact with his blistering-hot chili, and started thawing it in the microwave. Momma probably wouldn't have approved of anything short of a fresh home-cooked meal, but I wasn't planning on telling her, so we were good on that front. The microwave oven timer beeped at me, so I knew that our meal was nearly ready. One more cycle at full power, and we'd be ready to eat.

That was, if my husband made it home for dinner, which was anything but a given at this point in his investigation.

When Jake was working on a case, he tended to get consumed by it, and I didn't see why Harley's murder would be any different. Just in case, I grabbed my phone and called him.

He picked up on the second ring, which was a good sign.

"Hey, Jake. Any chance you'll be able to make it home for dinner?"

"I'm two minutes away," he said, and I could hear the smile in his voice. "If you don't feel like cooking, I'd be happy to thaw out some chili for us."

"As much as I appreciate the offer, the lasagna is almost ready." I'd dodged a bullet with my preemptive dinner strike, but I had to be careful not to let it show in my voice.

"That sounds great, too," he said, his cheeriness fading a little. I knew that he enjoyed my cooking, but I was going to have to let him serve us chili again soon. If marriage was nothing else, it was compromise.

To make up for taking away his dining options, I got out some of the cheddar chive rolls that I'd made the same day I'd done the lasagna and thawed them after the lasagna was resting. The rolls were best fresh from the oven with gobs of melted butter on them, but they were pretty good thawed out as well, especially if the fresh version wasn't available. That would put a smile back on his face.

Jake walked into the cottage and paused at the door to take a deep breath. Before he could say anything, I asked, "Any word about George?"

"Would it be okay with you if I just stood here a second and took in that aroma?" he asked gently.

"Sorry," I said, and I took in a breath myself. The defrosted lasagna and bread filled the kitchen with such a delightful aroma that it was a shame no one had ever tried to bottle it. "Are you hungry?"

"I'm starving," he said. "I skipped lunch."

"You shouldn't do that," I said as I handed him an empty plate. He filled it with more food than I would have, and I tried to show some restraint as I put an oversized portion on mine.

I failed miserably. There was no way that I was going to be able to eat all that food, even if I skipped having a roll, which I wasn't about to do. Maybe I'd wrap up what was left and have it the next day. Putting part of my portion back into the pan never crossed my mind.

As we sat at the table and ate, I made it a point not to quiz Jake about his day. After all, he deserved a break from the case, and for that matter, so did I. I'd spent so much of my focus on Harley Boggess, and that was after a full day of working at the donut shop, that I'd had little time to do anything else. It was pleasant chatting with my husband without having any ulterior motive.

After we were finished, he grabbed both of our plates and carried them to the sink. That was the rule in our house: if you cooked, your spouse did the dishes, and yes, that included premade meals that were simply heated up. I grabbed the glasses and silverware and put them in with the plates. "Do you want a hand with those?" I asked him as I started putting the leftover lasagna into a container. Surprisingly, or not, there hadn't been enough left on my plate to bother with, despite my earlier belief.

"That would be great," he said.

We worked together, enjoying the time and each other's company, and soon enough, the task was complete and our kitchen was spotless again.

"Suzanne, I don't know how you do it," he asked as he hung the dish towel up to dry.

"It's not that bad. I took some of Momma's recipes and added a few tricks I learned from Angelica, and I made something new and unique of my own."

"As great as the meal was, I wasn't talking about the food."

"What, then?"

"You didn't say another word about George Morris, or the case at all, as soon as I asked you not to."

"Jake, you should know by now that I'm obedient, if I'm anything," I said with as straight a face as I could manage.

We both laughed at that so loudly that it was a wonder Grace didn't come knocking on our door to see what was so hilarious. My husband and I were good for each other, and there wasn't a day that I wasn't happy we'd come together, a much different state of mind than I'd had during my first marriage to Max.

"Well, you did a fine job keeping it in, and as a reward, I'm going to share a few things about the case that I've learned. Unless you want to go first."

"No, by all means. The floor is yours," I said as we walked into the living room and sat on the couch. I'd stoked the fire upon arriving, and we had a nice cheery blaze going now.

"I'm afraid it's going to be a short dissertation," he said glumly. "First off, there hasn't been any sign of George anywhere. I've notified my old office at State Police Headquarters that our mayor is missing but that it's nothing to be alarmed about yet."

"Was that a good idea?" I asked him. The last thing I wanted was his old boss getting his hands on April Springs again.

"Maybe not, but my force isn't big enough to conduct a statewide hunt," he said. "For all of the good it's done me. I looked over Harley's home and his office pretty thoroughly. There were a few things that might turn out to be clues, but nothing struck me initially."

"How about George's office?"

"It's clean," he said. "I've been talking to the mayor about putting security cameras in City Hall, but he hasn't shown the slightest bit of interest so far."

"I don't blame him," I said. "I hate the thought of someone watching me every time I go in and out of the building."

"Do you think I like it any better?" Jake asked. "I'm afraid that's the way the world is headed. Anyway, it's a moot point, at least as far as Harley's murder is concerned."

"Has the coroner examined the body yet?" I asked, since it was not information I would ordinarily be privy to.

"Not yet, but why do you ask? I've been working on the assumption that the letter opener wound was fatal. Is there something you know that I don't?"

"Not about that," I said. "I was just curious."

He frowned at me for a moment, and then he said, "Okay, now it's your turn."

"Grace, Momma, and I are working on this case together," I said, letting the words spill out. I wasn't sure that he'd approve, so I wanted to get that out front immediately.

"Excellent. It's about time you three joined forces," he said with the hint of a smile.

"Excuse me? Does that mean that you approve?" I couldn't believe his casual acceptance of the new circumstances.

"There are a couple of reasons I think it's a good idea," he said. "Your mother has contacts in this town that you and I can only dream about, and besides, maybe she'll be a calming influence on the two of you."

"Have you *met* my mother?" I asked him with a grin.

"Point taken. It still makes sense, since Harley is more in your mother's circle of acquaintances than yours."

"That's exactly how it's turning out," I said. "Grace and I spoke with Amber North and Nathaniel Bloom, while Momma and I interviewed Curtis Daniels and Megan Grey."

"Hold on a second. Why are they all on your list of suspects?

Curtis I understand, and even Nathaniel, but what about the women?"

"Harley was dating Amber, and Megan was in love with him."

"Did he know that?" Jake asked.

"He probably suspected it, but then yesterday she declared her undying love for him and confirmed it," I said.

"How did Harley react to that? Forget that. How about Amber?"

"Harley laughed in Megan's face, and Amber dismissed her as not being worthy of being considered a threat," I said.

"Wow, and here I thought everyone in town but the mayor loved Harley before this happened," Jake replied.

"We have more," I said, afraid that he might take it as an affront that my team had done so much better than his had.

"There are even more suspects than you've mentioned so far?" he asked incredulously.

"No, but we also managed to get alibis out of each of them, for what they were worth."

"Let's hear them," Jake said as he got out the little notebook he always carried with him.

I started talking, being sure to give him time to take notes. "Nathaniel claimed to be in his office all morning preparing for a meeting this afternoon. I'm not sure if it's true, but Seth Lancaster came by while we were there and confirmed it, so it's possible. Amber said that she was home alone watching television after nine thirty, which is what she was doing when Grace and I showed up on her doorstep this afternoon. Megan claimed that she was at work in Admissions at the hospital, but she could have easily slipped out while no one was looking. They have security cameras there, don't they?"

Jake nodded. "In the emergency room and at the front desk, but not anywhere near the Admin offices."

I frowned for a second. "How about the parking lot?"

"Just the one that's open to the public. I had reason to inquire last month over another matter. That's why I know."

"What was it about?"

"Sorry, I can't talk about it," Jake said. "I already know Curtis's alibi, and his secretary's, too."

"We didn't even list Wendy as a suspect," I admitted. "Do you think she might have done it?"

"At this point, I'm still gathering information. Who knows? Maybe Harley hit on her and she fought back. They had proximity going for them, which is enough in and of itself sometimes if there was bad blood between them."

"Was there?"

"I couldn't say, since I'm still looking into it. Anyway, her alibi is that she was alone at the office all morning, while Curtis was out looking at some of their property assets he was considering liquidating." Wendy's name was going on our list. I couldn't believe that Momma, Grace, and I had not even considered her as a potential killer.

"Jake, I hope we didn't cross any lines today."

"Suzanne, ordinarily I might say that you had, but I can use all of the help that I can get on this one. Half my deputies are out sick, and the other half are scrambling to cover basic services. This is probably the worst possible time to be conducting a murder investigation."

"I'm sure if Harley were still around, he'd agree with you wholeheartedly," I said, raising an eyebrow as I did so.

"I know it's not very politic to say it, but there's nobody here but the two of us."

"I get that," I said as I patted his shoulder gently. My crack had been undeserved. The massage was my way of apologizing, and Jake had readily accepted. It was part of our unspoken language that many good marriages possessed.

"Where does that leave us now?" I asked him.

"I don't know about you and your crack team, but I have to go back to the office," he said reluctantly as he stood and stretched.

"Can't the investigation wait until morning?" I asked him.

"Probably not, but that's not why I'm going back in. Stephen and I are going to patrol in a squad car together tonight. He's good company, though not as good as you are."

"He'd better not be. Wouldn't it be more efficient if you each took a car?"

"Yes, but I feel better at night when there are two officers in each car," he said. "It's my rule, and I don't think it sets a very good precedent if I'm the first one who breaks it."

"I understand that. Should I wait up for you?"

"With your hours? You'd better not. I just hope I'm back by the time you leave for work in the morning. You *are* going in to the donut shop, aren't you?"

"Yes, it's not my turn to get a few days off again yet," I said. My assistant, Emma Blake, and her mother were running Donut Hearts two days a week to give me more time with Jake, but their time at the helm was still four days away. I didn't mind, though. I loved my shop, and I wasn't entirely sure that the arrangement was working for me. After all, Jake still had a more-than-full-time job, and it left me with too much time on my hands, especially when he had to go in on his days off. Maybe when and if he ever retired, I'd sell the shop to Emma and her mother if they were interested, but that was probably a long way off. In the meantime, I was going to enjoy every second I had making donuts for the nice folks of April Springs.

I thought about calling Grace or even Momma after Jake left, but something held me back. In the end, I decided to spend my last few hours before bed enjoying the fire, a good book, and my own company. I loved my husband dearly, but I still enjoyed a little time alone every now and then.

CHAPTER 12

"HAVEN'T YOU BEEN TO BED yet?" I asked Jake as I came into the kitchen after sleeping fitfully in the time I had. He was nursing a cup of coffee and frowning when I approached him, but he did his best to smile when I walked into the room.

"What can I say? It's been a long day," he said.

"Have you been able to make any progress?"

"Not that you'd notice," he said. "Is it time to make the donuts already?"

"It's always time," I said with a smile. "I don't know how you do it, Jake."

"Do what, stay awake this late?"

"No, deal with people all day long you suspect of being possible murderers. How do you not see the worst in everyone you meet?"

"The truth of the matter is that I believe that most people are fundamentally good," he said after a moment's pause. "Certainly there are evil folks in this world, I'm not naïve about that, but for most killers, the act is an irrational one, dictated by their circumstances, whether real or imagined. I've often said that given the right conditions, anyone could be a killer, but the obverse of that is true, too. Given the perfect setting, just about anyone can do the right thing, too."

"You're a complicated man. You know that, don't you?" I asked him after I leaned forward and kissed his cheek.

"I've been called much worse, even today," he said.

"Who's been giving you a hard time?"

"I tend to make people uncomfortable with the questions I have to ask them."

"I understand how that feels completely," I answered. "At least you get paid to do it."

"Why do you do it, Suzanne? I suddenly realize that I never asked you that question before. Is it out of a sense of justice for the victim, or do you just hate seeing wrongs go unpunished?"

"Can't it be a little of both, with some other factors thrown in, too?"

He laughed a little at that. "And you're calling me complicated?"

"Hey, it's just who I am. You knew that when you married me."

"I wasn't complaining," he said as he took another sip of coffee. "That's one of the things I find most attractive about you."

"What are some of the others?" I asked coyly.

He swatted my behind. "It's too early to be fishing for compliments, young lady."

"It's never too early, as far as I'm concerned," I replied with a laugh of my own. "I'll see you later."

"Have a good day."

"Hey, I'm spending the morning making donuts that just about the entire town will be enjoying later. What's not to like about that?"

"If you say so. You don't know how I do my job, but I'd go crazy in a week if I had to do yours."

"More likely a day," I said with a smile.

It was rare when Jake was awake when I left for work, and it always picked up my spirits. I loved him, but it was more than that. I genuinely liked the man, something that seemed to be in rare supply in too many married couples. Then again, though neither of us was exactly young anymore, our marriage still was, and we were in the honeymoon phase of our union.

May it last forever and a day, as far as I was concerned.

The Jeep was freezing when I got in, so I warmed it up for a few minutes as I scraped the frost off the windshield. I loved cold weather, but every now and then, I wouldn't have minded having a garage.

The short drive to Donut Hearts was uneventful, and as I walked in, I felt embraced by the warmth of the place. We'd had our furnace repaired the winter before, so it was nice having convenient and consistent heat. Flipping on a few light switches and the coffee pot as I walked into the kitchen, I turned the fryer on to give it a chance to come to temperature as well. Taking out my trusty recipe book, I opened it to my basic cake donut recipe, though I knew it by heart. It was nice having it there as a reference, a comfort in its mere presence. Measuring out the flour and other ingredients, I found myself humming softly to myself as I worked. I loved having Emma around, but this was my favorite time of morning at the shop, when most of the world around me slept and I worked to brighten some of their days with what I offered. I never claimed that my donuts were nutritional, but then again, I didn't advocate a steady diet of them, either. They were meant to be a treat, a present my customers could give themselves without any need for a reason, and that suited me just fine.

I was dropping the last of my new pumpkin apple spice donuts into the hot oil when Emma started to come in. She was a little late, but I was in such a good mood that I didn't mind. "Oops.

Four minutes later, after I pulled the last of the donuts from the oil, I pushed the kitchen door aside. "All clear," I said as I started icing them, getting the glaze on the donuts before they had a chance to cool.

"Sorry I'm late," she said as she put her jacket on the coatrack and donned her apron. "My car wouldn't start, so I had to get Dad to give me a ride."

"I bet he loved getting out of a warm bed to do that," I said.

"Are you kidding? He's been up all night getting ready to put a special edition out. I'm not sure what he's going to write, but I saw a glimpse of his headline."

"What does it say?" I asked as I moved the donuts to a drip rack before I placed them on trays.

"Murder Hits Home Again."

"That's not bad," I said.

"You should have seen some of the ones he crossed out. Councilman Killed in Mayor's Chair, Harley's Homicide, and my favorite, No One Is Safe From The April Springs Killer."

"That's a little long for a headline, isn't it?" I asked as I shook my head. None of them had surprised me. Ray Blake's little newspaper was mostly a flyer for store ads and classifieds, but he aspired to be an investigative reporter, and sometimes it showed a little too clearly in the issues he published.

"That's the only reason he killed it," she said. "Is the rumor I heard true?"

"Which rumor might that be?" I asked her, careful not to say too much.

"That George is on the run," she said.

"Not as far as I know."

"But he's missing, right?"

"I don't know if you could say that he's missing," I said carefully.

"But you don't know where he is."

"Who's asking, my assistant or the newspaper publisher's daughter?" Emma and I walked a fine line when we discussed my investigations, and we'd learned, through painful trial and error, when not to cross it.

"Suzanne, I promise you that this is all strictly off the record," she said earnestly. "I never discuss our conversations with my father in any way, shape, or form anymore."

"I know that," I said. "George isn't in town, but that doesn't mean that he had anything to do with Harley's murder, no matter how it might look."

"I don't think he did it, either," she said. "Are you and Grace digging into Harley's homicide, since it ties in so closely with the mayor? I know how close you all are."

"We might be," I said.

"Good," Emma answered. "George Morris is a good guy in my book, and a great mayor. I'd hate to see this ruin him when it wasn't his fault."

"I would, too," I said.

Emma sighed, and then she looked at the dishes I'd already piled up for her. "Well, those bowls aren't going to wash themselves, are they? This morning, I'm kind of looking forward to burying my hands in some hot and soapy water."

"See what you can do in twenty minutes," I said. "By then I'll have the yeast dough ready for its first raise and we can take our break outside, if it's not too cold for you this morning."

"I wouldn't let a little chill in the air stop me," she said, "and you know it."

We enjoyed our break outside, but soon enough, it was time to go back in and continue the process of making our yeast donuts.

I'd had my eye on a new cutter that cut out donuts in the shape of Christmas wreaths, but I'd lost the online auction for it. On a lark, I'd bid on one that made Santas, but they hadn't turned out as well as I'd hoped. Maybe I'd try again in July, when the seasonal cutters weren't such a hot item, if anyone had one for sale. Finally, two minutes before we were set to open shop for the day, I was adjusting the last tray in the display case, having just finished setting up the cash register, when there was a knock at our front door. Ever since I'd pushed my opening to seven, folks got impatient for me to let them in, and on cold mornings like we were experiencing now, I knew that I wouldn't be able to refuse anyone's plea for sanctuary from the chill.

I wasn't expecting to see who was standing out there tapping, though.

Grinning as though he didn't have a care in the world was our missing mayor himself, George Morris.

"Where on earth have you been?" I asked George as I opened the door to let him in.

"I was visiting a friend of mine at his lake cabin in the mountains. Moose and I have been buddies for a long time. He called me out of the blue yesterday to invite me up there, and since I didn't have anything pressing, I joined him for some good food and even better lies."

"Have you spoken to anyone in town since you got back?" I asked him.

"No, I drove straight here to get some donuts for breakfast. Moose is a fine short-order cook, but I knew if I had breakfast with him, I wouldn't be able to move for a while." He peered at the donuts behind me. "I see an old-fashioned donut that has my name on it."

"There's no time to eat," I said. "George, you're in trouble."

"Why is that?" he asked me as he kept looking longingly at the treats behind the counter.

"Somebody killed Harley Boggess yesterday morning in your chair in City Hall with your letter opener."

"Not funny, Suzanne," he said. "Should I serve myself, or are you going to get that donut for me? You know what? Why don't you make it two? I'm feeling pretty great this morning."

"Sorry to ruin your good mood, but I wasn't kidding."

George's grin froze on his face for a moment before he spoke again. "Are you serious?"

"I wish I weren't, but it's true."

"What happened?" he asked me.

"That's what everyone wants to know. Should I call Jake, or do you want to?"

"I'll do it," George said. "I can't believe this. I play hooky for one day, and look what happens."

"Some folks are saying that you might have done it yourself," I told him as he fumbled for his cellphone.

"Of course they are. You don't think so, do you?"

"George, you are many things, but a killer isn't one of them. Besides, if you had done it, you certainly wouldn't have run away."

"Who says I was running anywhere?"

"There was an anonymous tip," I said.

"I'll just bet there was, from the killer, more likely than not." He dialed my husband's number, and then he said, "Jake, it's George. I'm at Donut Hearts. Suzanne just gave me the bare bones of what happened. Should I come over there, do you want to meet me here, or should I head straight to your office? Okay. Sure." He stopped and glanced at me. "I can do that. I'll tell her." He hung up and turned to me. "He says that I should wait in back."

"That might be a problem," I said, thinking of Emma and

her likely impulse to call her dad to tell him that the mayor was back.

"What's the matter, are you afraid of harboring a fugitive?" George asked with a grin.

"It's Emma. Give me one second."

"Okay, but I don't know how long I should stand here. Your customers will be coming in soon."

"Just don't go anywhere."

I walked into the kitchen and approached Emma, who was still working on the latest batch of dishes. "I need you to do something for me and not tell anyone about it, most especially your father."

"If there's a body that needs burying, I'm your gal. Do you want me to hold the flashlight, or should I start shoveling?"

"Emma, this is serious. George Morris just showed up. He's out front, and until I told him what happened, he had no idea that Harley had been murdered. I need you to cover the front and not tell anyone that he's back here, most especially your father. Can you do that for me?"

"Of course I can," she said, her expression suddenly solemn.

That was good enough for me.

"George, come on back," I said.

He'd found the time to stop and grab a donut on the way. "Seriously?"

"I'll pay you for it, but I'm hungry," he said. "Hi, Emma."

"Hello, Mr. Mayor. I'm glad you're okay."

"Why wouldn't I be?" he asked her, genuinely surprised by her statement.

"Something happened to Harley Boggess yesterday. I just didn't want it happening to you, too."

"I appreciate that, young lady," he said.

"Emma, when Jake gets here, send him straight back."

"Will do," she said.

"She's a good girl," George said after she was gone.

"Despite who her father is?"

"It's not as bad as all that. Ray provides a service to the community, no matter whether I agree with his reporting or not."

"Let's hear you say that after you read today's paper," I said.

That brought a look of alarm to his face. "Why, what's he going to say?"

"I have no clue, but given the circumstances, can you imagine any scenario where it's good?"

"No, not really."

"George, I have to ask. Did you see Harley yesterday before you left town?"

The mayor frowned as he nodded. "He's about the only person I did speak to. He barged into my office spouting off about how he was going to bury me in the next election, and I told him he couldn't get elected dogcatcher if only the cats were allowed to vote. He stormed out, Moose called me, and I decided that I'd had enough, so I took off. At that moment, Harley could have had my job wrapped in a ribbon, but I didn't kill him."

"So, who did?" I asked him.

"I have no idea," George said. After a moment, he added, "Hang on. He's been arguing with Nathaniel Bloom in our meetings lately, and by the way Harley's been acting, there's a woman making his life more difficult than it already was or I'll eat my hat. I don't have a clue who she might be, though."

"It's Amber North," I said.

"No. Really? Amber? Why?"

"I'm sure that some men must see her charm," I said.

"Well, I'm certainly not one of them. Wow. Harley and Amber. Go figure." He frowned a moment as he looked at me. "You're digging into this, aren't you?"

"With a little help, yes, I am."

"Suzanne, tell me it's not because of me."

"I can't do that," I said, meeting his steady gaze with one of my own.

"Your mother is going to kill me," George said. "She's been trying to get you to back off with your investigations for years."

"Funny, she's helping us out this time," I said.

"Why on earth would she do that?"

"She cares for you, George, and she doesn't want to see this undo your political career."

"She just doesn't want to have to step in and take the job over," the mayor said after he bit his lower lip.

"We both know better than that. Before Jake gets here, is there anything else I need to know?"

"Not that I can think of," he said. "How does Jake feel about you nosing around in his case?"

"As long as I stay out of his way, he's okay with it," I answered as the kitchen door opened suddenly.

It had better be Jake, or there was going to be a problem.

If Ray Blake came in, he and his daughter would be escorted off the premises immediately, and I'd be in the market for a new assistant. I couldn't have loved Emma more if she'd been my own daughter, but divulging what I'd just told her not to would be grounds for immediate dismissal, no matter how much it would have broken my heart to do it.

Thankfully, it was my husband, and from the expression on his face, he wasn't particularly happy about the situation at the moment.

I had a hunch that things were only about to get worse.

CHAPTER 13

"How long have you been here, George?" Jake asked him pointedly.

"I just got back into town not ten minutes ago."

He glanced at me, and I nodded. "That's true, as far as I know. I had to tell him about Harley."

"I wish you'd have let me do that, Suzanne," my husband said.

"He didn't know before I told him, Jake. Trust me."

"Let me get this straight. Do you actually think that I killed him?" George asked as he looked incredulously at my husband.

"George, you were a cop once yourself. Think about it, and then tell me how you'd look at the situation objectively."

The mayor frowned for a moment, and then he nodded. "Truth be told, I'd probably lock me up."

"That's not going to happen though, not unless you did it."

"*Saying* that I'm innocent is pretty worthless, isn't it?" he asked.

"Not to me," Jake said. "Let's go somewhere and figure out how you fit into this." He turned to me. "Nobody's outside waiting to get in, but we can't hang around much longer. Suzanne, we'll talk later."

"Sounds good. Now go."

I walked out with them, and after the two of them made it safely outside without being seen, I turned to Emma. "Thanks for not calling your father."

"Susanne, I would never betray your trust like that. You asked me to keep it quiet, and that's what I'll do." She hesitated a second, and then she asked, "Exactly how long does that have to be?"

"I'd rather you didn't say anything about this happening at all."

Emma nodded. "Consider it done."

Hillary Teal, the older woman who often made costumes for Max's seniors' theater group, came in. "Suzanne, did I just see your husband with the mayor?"

"I don't know, did you?" I asked her, trying not to give anything away.

"I don't honestly know myself. I really must go see Dr. Sedgewick. I believe my eyesight is getting worse by the minute."

"What can I do for you, Hillary?"

"I'll take a dozen of your most deadly donuts, dear," she said with a grin. "The girls and I are having a little party, and they all so love your tasty treats."

"I'm honored," I said as I put together a nice selection. After I took her money and made change, I asked, "Are there any new plays on the horizon?"

"I've been meaning to ask Max that very question. He's so in love these days that there's not as much time for us anymore." Her face reddened for a moment as she quickly added, "That was rather tacky of me, wasn't it?"

"No worries on my account. I'm happy for Max. He found Emily, and what's even better, she found him. It's hard enough in this world to find someone you belong with, so I won't begrudge either of them their happiness. After all, if Max hadn't cheated on me, I never would have found Jake."

"You are wise beyond your years, Suzanne Hart." With a twinkle in her eye, she added, "But not beyond mine."

"Well, I hope there will be time enough for me to get there, too."

The donuts were selling briskly, and I was already out of my latest experiment of pumpkin apple spice treats. I might just have a winner on my hands, but one day's sales weren't enough to give me reason to put it in the rotation of my offerings. I'd have to have at least two more successful runs before it made the grade. I was just returning from the kitchen after dropping off the empty tray to Emma for a sound cleaning when I saw someone unexpected waiting for me at the counter out front.

Nathaniel Bloom was paying a visit to my donut shop, something that was definitely out of the norm for him.

"Good morning. What can I do for you, Councilman?"

"Nathaniel will do just fine," he said. "I've got a meeting in an hour, and I thought a dozen donuts might make for a nice change of pace from our usual fare."

"You came to the right place, then," I said as I grabbed an empty box. "Do you want anything in particular?"

"Let's make it half a dozen plain glazed, and you can pick out the rest."

"I can do that," I said as I chose some of my slower sellers to fill out his dozen. He shouldn't mind, since he had made it my choice, and besides, he was one of my suspects. If he was a cold-blooded killer, I didn't feel good about giving him the best I had to offer. It might have been petty, but I could live with myself doing it, especially since I never sold *anything* that I wouldn't eat myself. "We don't see you around here all that much," I said as I collected his donuts.

"I realize that, and I decided it was high time I changed

that," he said with a grin. The man was a born politician, and I wondered if his ambitions were strictly local. Had Harley known something that would have prevented Nathaniel from going after a bigger and better office sometime down the road? If he had, it wouldn't be impossible to believe that Nathaniel might try to remove the stumbling block sooner rather than later. "How's the investigation going?" he asked me casually.

"You'll have to ask my husband about that," I said after I told him the cost of the donuts.

As he paid me, he said, "I was talking about the unofficial one you are conducting."

"We're making progress," I said. It wasn't a total fabrication. Grace and I had managed to accrue five suspects in less than twenty-four hours, which was quite an accomplishment, at least in my book.

"Do you have any strong leads yet?" he asked me. "I bet you're leaning toward Amber North, aren't you?"

There was no one else in Donut Hearts at the moment, so Nathaniel clearly felt free to talk.

"She's on our list," I said as I made change.

"But the mayor is probably at the top, isn't he?"

"Why do you say that?" I asked him without letting on that I knew more than he did about the situation.

"Come on. It's obvious, isn't it? Harley was murdered in George's office with his letter opener, and the mayor is gone. How much clearer does it need to be?"

"It so happens the mayor is back in town, and he has an airtight alibi," I said. Why had I just told him that? For one thing, I didn't want anyone to know that George was back in town, and for another, I had no idea if his alibi was any good or not. It was just that Nathaniel had been so smug and certain about George's presumed guilt that I couldn't let it pass without comment. Doing so would have felt disloyal to him somehow.

It suddenly dawned on me that I was no better than Momma or Grace, and most likely, I owed each woman a heartfelt apology.

Nathaniel was clearly surprised to hear the news. "How can you possibly know that?"

"He came by here first thing this morning and cleared it all up with Jake," I answered, hoping that it was indeed true.

"Interesting," Nathaniel said as he absently picked up the box of donuts. "I suppose that I'll see you later, Suzanne."

"You can count on it," I replied.

Nathaniel looked at me for an instant with something a great deal less than warmth, but then it was quickly gone. With a smile that felt quite a bit less sincere than he must have meant it to, the councilman left Donut Hearts. I'd been rash telling him about George and his alibi, but it was a sin I could live with. After all, defending a friend was never a bad thing to do, at least as far as I was concerned.

Promptly at ten, the ladies from my book club arrived. It was always a pleasure meeting with them, even if I happened to be in the midst of a murder investigation occasionally. "Emma, they're here," I said as I called back into the kitchen.

She'd been warned about the impending meeting earlier, so she was ready to work the front while I spent a pleasant half hour discussing our latest book. Jennifer, an elegant redhead who was our leader, approached the counter. "Don't forget, this one's on me," she said as she put her customary fifty-dollar bill on the counter. I'd given up trying to make change for her, as it had only left us both feeling less than happy about the exchange. "You're too good to me, Jennifer."

"Don't kid yourself, Suzanne. Your treats are worth every penny."

"What would you ladies like today?" I asked the three of

them as they clustered around the front. Jennifer had been joined by our other two members, Hazel and Elizabeth. Hazel was on a perpetual diet, so I knew she'd be ordering as lightly as possible, so she surprised me by saying, "I'll have four bearclaws, please. I don't know what the rest of you want."

"Hazel, what's wrong?"

"My husband is having an affair," she said, and then she started softly crying.

"I'm so sorry," was all that I could manage to say.

"She doesn't know for a fact that he's cheating on her," Elizabeth said.

"Why else would he work late every night with that cute young secretary he just hired?" Hazel asked.

"Maybe we should cancel the meeting today," I suggested.

"No, please don't," Hazel said. "Right now, you three are all I've got."

Jennifer frowned a bit, and then she said, "Hazel, we're not going to stand by and watch you destroy all of your hard work dieting and exercising. You may have one treat, just like the rest of us."

I wasn't at all certain how Hazel would react to the edict, but she stopped crying, dabbed at her eyes, and then nodded in agreement. "You're right. He's not worth it."

"That's the spirit," Elizabeth said. "Now that you mention it, a bearclaw sounds great to me, too."

"Elizabeth," Jennifer chastised her.

"What? It does. Besides, I'm only getting one."

I put three bearclaws on individual plates.

"I just asked for one," Elizabeth said.

"I'm having one, too," I said. It was time for me to indulge a little myself.

"You might as well make it four," Jennifer said with a sigh. After I plated the last one, she carried the tray to our favorite couch and chairs, since she was the official hostess for the meeting, while I grabbed our coffees. Once we were settled in and we'd enjoyed our treats, Hazel asked, "Shall we get started?"

"If you're sure that you're up to it?" I asked her.

"That's why we're here, is it not? Let's talk about *Killing the Publisher.*"

"I'm getting awfully tired of these mysteries where the main character is a writer. Don't these people have any imagination at all?" Jennifer asked.

"It's how they spend their lives, sitting in rooms by themselves making things up. What else would you have them do?" Hazel asked.

"Not the ones who have co-authors," Elizabeth said.

"They probably still don't get out much," I said. "Besides, there have been plenty of mystery writers on TV for quite a while."

"I love Castle," Hazel said. "He's so cute."

"I'm an Ellery Queen fan myself," I said. "I never miss a Jim Hutton marathon."

"Maybe I spoke a little hastily," Jennifer said. "I still watch *Murder She Wrote* every time I catch a rerun. At least this book was cleverly plotted; I'll give Gwendolyn Fry that much. She's really good, isn't she? I thought her publisher was a really nasty fellow."

I looked over and saw that Elizabeth was grinning. "What's so funny?"

"You should hear the story of how the book came to be," Elizabeth said smugly. She prided herself on being able to find the most private email addresses of our authors and often had correspondences with them.

"Tell us," Hazel said eagerly. It was good to see her excited about something, anything.

"Well, it seems she wanted to get out of her contract, but

her publisher wouldn't let her. She owed them one more book, and even though she offered to return her advance, he refused. So what did she do?"

"She killed him in the book," I said with a grin of my own. It sounded like something that I might do, if I had a fingernail of the combined talent, determination, and luck that most authors had.

"That's exactly what she did," Elizabeth said, crowing about it. "I looked up the man online and saw that she had portrayed his physical attributes perfectly, though of course she changed the man's name. I have a hunch that a great many folks still recognized him, though."

"That explains why she spent so much time describing his death so graphically. I thought she crossed the line for a cozy mystery."

"The line is getting blurrier every day," Hazel said, caught up in our discussion and forgetting about her own woes for a moment. "I've seen some themes lately that made me downright queasy."

"If you think mysteries are bad, then stay out of the young adult section," Jennifer said. "I'm a grown woman, and some of those topics make me blush."

"The irony is that the book was so successful, the publisher had no choice but to ask for more."

"I hope she said no," Hazel said.

"As a matter of fact, she got double her last advance. She told me in secret that she's killing a former agent of a friend of hers next. Evidently the woman collected some of her foreign rights royalties and neglected to pass them on. I wouldn't want to be her enemy."

"I would think that a mystery writer would make a bad adversary," Jennifer said.

"Why is that?" I asked her.

"Think about it. They sit around all day trying to come up with new ways to kill people," she said. "Is that someone you'd want out to get you?"

"No, not when you put it that way."

Hazel's cellphone rang, and I knew that she must have forgotten to turn off the ringer, since it was one of our club's hard-and-fast rules. "Sorry," she said as she glanced at who was calling her. "It's him," she said with distaste.

"Ignore it," Elizabeth said.

"What could it hurt to see what he wants?" I asked. I hated the thought that Hazel's world was turning upside down, and the last thing I wanted to happen was for her to give up without a fight.

"I might as well." After answering it, she said, "Yes? I'm with my book club. What? When? Now? Okay. Yes."

Her face had transformed during the conversation, going from cloudy to nothing but sun by the end of it. "I've been such a fool," she said when she turned back to us.

"What's going on?" I asked her.

"My dear husband has been working late so he can make the time to take me on a romantic getaway. It was all in my imagination."

"What about his cute new secretary?" Jennifer asked her.

"She and her husband have been trying to get pregnant for a year, and it finally happened, so she's trying to get in extra hours before the baby comes. Do you mind if I duck out early?"

"No, we completely understand," Jennifer said.

"Elizabeth, I hate to ask, but you're my ride."

"It's fine with me. Let's go."

After the two of them left, Jennifer said, "I don't suppose there's any reason to continue our discussion, is there?"

"I'd be happy to chat with you about anything that's on your mind," I said as I glanced at my watch. "For another twelve minutes, at any rate."

"I don't know how you do it, Suzanne."

"What's that?"

"Run this shop, have a life outside of Donut Hearts, and still manage to join our little group."

She didn't know the half of it. "I'm often tired but rarely bored," I said with a grin.

"I envy you that," she said.

"Is there something you'd like to talk about?" Something was clearly troubling her, and if I could help, I wanted to.

Jennifer wanted to tell me, I could see it in her eyes, but finally she patted my hand as she said, "I'm fine. Just being a little wistful, that's all."

"I'm here if you need me," I said. "Being my friend isn't a conditional thing."

"I understand that, and believe me, it's greatly appreciated."

She stood, gave me a quick hug, and then she left the shop. I wished that she'd confided in me, but when the time was right, I'd be there for her if she needed me. In the meantime, I needed to give her some space. It wasn't like I didn't have anything else to do.

After all, I still had a murder to solve and not a great deal of time to accomplish it in.

CHAPTER 14

"Hi, Suzanne," Megan Gray surprised me by saying just before I was ready to close up for the day. We'd nearly sold out of donuts, and the coffee was probably fit only to clean out our drains.

"Sorry I don't have much of a selection," I said as I pointed to the display case behind me.

"That's okay, I'm not here for donuts."

"Is there something that I can do for you?" I asked her, reaching for my cellphone just in case I needed to call for help in a hurry. Megan didn't appear to pose a threat, but I'd never gone wrong overestimating one of my suspects' capacity for violence, no matter how unlikely it seemed at the time.

"I've been thinking about our conversation before," she said. "I know you suspect that I did something to Harley, and I'm here to convince you that I didn't kill him. How can I do that?"

"You can give me a better alibi," I said.

"I was at work. I already told you that!" The mouse was roaring a little, and Emma must have heard her.

She came out of the kitchen and looked suspiciously at my guest as she asked, "Is everything okay out here?"

"It's fine," I said, though I wasn't entirely sure that was the case at all. "There are just a few more trays and mugs out here, and then we'll be finished for the day."

Emma gathered them up, but I noticed that she left the kitchen door ajar so she could keep tabs on me as she worked. I didn't even mind if she eavesdropped on this conversation, since it might just save my life.

"Megan," I said in a calm voice, "there's no reason to be that upset."

"You try being a murder suspect and see how you like it."

"I have been myself, so I know that it isn't pleasant, but then again, I also knew that I was innocent at the time, so I wasn't all that worried about it." That wasn't strictly true, but I was trying to push her a little to see if she'd crack. It might not have been the wisest strategy in the world, but sometimes I had to take a risk in order to make something happen. Besides, Emma was just in the next room, for all of the good that might do me. I glanced over at the kitchen door. I could see in a little, but Megan couldn't see her at all, given the angle where she stood. Emma was there all right, but she wasn't doing dishes. Instead, she was holding our weapon of choice when it came to self-defense, the store's aluminum softball bat. It should have been behind the counter with me, but somehow it had ended up back there with her. Maybe I should buy another bat so we'd have one for each spot, if I made it out of this alive. Regardless, it felt good having Emma there as backup, so I decided to push a little harder if the opportunity presented itself.

My explanation seemed to mollify Megan a little. "Suzanne, you've seen my office. I work by myself all day long. I suppose I could slip away and no one would notice, but the truth of the matter is that I didn't. I worked all morning, and I never left hospital grounds."

"Without a decent alibi, and given your rebuffed declaration of love for Harley, what else can people think?" I asked her. "You honestly can't blame me for considering you a suspect."

"Suzanne, haven't you ever had an all-consuming crush in your life, where you idolized someone who didn't deserve it, only you were too blind and lonely at the time to see it? When

Harley laughed in my face, it was as though a veil had been ripped from my eyes, and for the first time in a very long time, I could see clearly again. I know most folks think I'm this quiet, mousy woman, but I live a full and robust life in my mind. When I'm reading my novels, I come alive in them, becoming the person I'm normally too shy to share with anyone else in real life."

I did know how she felt, and it tugged at my heart. If Megan had been going for my sympathy, it was working. There had been a particular boy in high school, Pat McKinley, I'd been so smitten with that I could barely breathe whenever I was around him. That went on for an uncomfortably long time, until I heard him making fun of my obvious devotion with some of his friends when he didn't know I was around. I'd undergone the exact same experience that Megan was describing, and Pat had been dead to me for the rest of school. "Megan, I sympathize, I truly do, but I'm just trying to find Harley's killer."

"I suppose I understand that," she said, clearly hoping for a different outcome. "You should know something about me. I'm going to change, Suzanne. As much as I love my books, I'm going to start living my real life on my own terms, as bravely as I do in my imagination. This shyness and insecurity I've been feeling my entire life ends right here and now."

"All I can say is that I wish you luck, and I mean that sincerely." I glanced at the remaining donuts, now resting in a half-empty box. "Would you like some treats, on the house?"

"Sure, why not?" she asked with a smile. It was the first time I'd seen her with a full-blown smile, and I could start to see that she was being completely sincere. I just hoped that she didn't turn out to be the killer, because if she was, I'd still have to nail her all the same for her crime, no matter how much she'd gotten to me.

Once Megan was gone, Emma came out, still carrying the softball bat. "What was that all about, or should I even ask?"

"The truth of the matter is that it was either a courageous act of openness and honesty, or it was an attempt to win my sympathy in order to divert my suspicion from her in Harley's murder," I said without thinking about who I was telling. "That's off the record, by the way."

"Of course it is," Emma said. "Do you have any idea who killed Harley?"

"I honestly don't have a clue," I said as I handed her the last tray. "We can close up a little early today. As soon as you finish with the dishes, you can take off."

"What about cleaning the tables and sweeping the floor out here?"

"I've got enough time to do that myself," I said. Honestly, I didn't mind doing the work. I wanted a little time to process what I'd just learned. It was a fair question Emma had posed. Which scenario did I really believe? After she left Donut Hearts, I was no closer to reaching a conclusion than I had been before, and I still wasn't sure by the time I'd finished cashing out the register and cleaning the front.

There was a tap at the front door just as I shut off the main lights, and I was kind of surprised when I looked up to see Momma standing outside.

"Was I expecting you?" I asked her as I let her in.

She looked disappointed. "I thought we were sleuthing together today. Why, has something else come up?"

"No," I said after I let her in and closed the door behind her, being sure to lock it securely before I turned back to her. "As a matter of fact, I just had an interesting visit from one of our suspects."

"I'm dying to hear who it was," she said just as my cellphone rang.

"Hang on one second." It was Grace. "Where are you?" I asked her.

"That's the thing. I'm going to be late. Can you think of some way to occupy yourself for a few hours without getting yourself into trouble?"

"Momma's here with me," I said.

"That doesn't answer my question," she said with a laugh.

"Is everything all right?"

"Yes, I've just got a rep who's gotten herself into a jam, and I'm trying to help her figure a way out of it. From the sound of things, it might take a while."

"Is it work related?" I asked.

"No, the silly nit's been dating two men without telling either one about the other, and last night while she was stacking two dates on top of each other, they proposed."

"Together?" I asked, shaking my head in disbelief. I knew there were women who could date a variety of men at the same time, but I'd never been one of them. I seemed to have it coded in my DNA that I could only be with one man at a time.

"Of course not. I just said that they didn't know about each other. That's not the real problem, though."

"I'd love to hear what it is, if that's just the lead-up," I told her.

"She said yes to both of them," Grace said.

"You're kidding."

"I wish I were, but you can't make things like this up."

"Stay with her as long as you need to," I said. "I don't envy you."

"Yes, I've got to admit, I'd rather be there with you than dealing with this mess. Well, I'd better get back inside before she melts down completely."

"Good luck," I said.

"Right back at you."

"What was that all about?" Momma asked me, a look of concern spread across her face.

"Grace is helping one of her workers with a personal problem," I said, and then I repeated what she'd just told me.

"So I gathered from your end of the conversation. Did the daft woman honestly just accept marriage proposals from two men? How does something like that even happen?"

"I'm not quite sure myself, but it seems that's the case," I said.

"The answer is easy enough," Momma said.

"I'm listening," I replied, eager to hear my mother's take on the situation.

"Tell Grace to have the woman flip a coin, making one man heads and the other tails."

"Seriously? That's your great advice, flipping a coin? It seems kind of random, if you ask me."

"Suzanne, think about it. The results of the coin flip don't actually matter."

"Now I'm really lost."

"Have her flip the coin, and then, just as she learns the outcome, have Grace ask her if she's happy with the result or disappointed. That might not tell her which man to marry, but it will certainly point her in the right direction."

"Momma, you're brilliant."

"So I've been told. Well, stop nattering away with me. Call her back."

I did as she suggested, and to my chagrin, Grace got it immediately. "Give your mother a hug for me," she said.

"You can do it yourself later," I said. "While you're gone, Momma and I are going to go talk to some of our suspects again."

"Just save at least one for me," she said.

"I promise."

After I hung up, I turned back to Momma. "How did you happen to think of that?"

"I do it sometimes myself when I'm faced with a difficult decision," she said. "It's amazing how often it works. Now, who should we tackle first?"

I told her about Megan's visit, and Momma nodded. "I can understand her reaction completely."

"Momma, was there a Harley in your life at one time? No, of course not. Forget I even asked you that question."

"Jason Henderson," she said without hesitation. "Believe it or not, I haven't always been the self-confident woman you know and love. Jason knew every button to push to get me to adore him in junior high school, and yet he didn't return a single ounce of my affection."

"Did he end up breaking your heart?" I asked, seeing my mother in a new light.

"No, actually I broke his nose," Momma said.

"Seriously? You punched him in the snout?" I knew that my mother could be rowdy at times, but physical violence against a boy who didn't return her affections seemed a bit extreme, even for her.

"Of course not. Don't be silly, Suzanne. I accidentally opened a classroom door, and he happened to be standing on the other side of it. It smacked him squarely in the face, and he cried like a little girl. After that, I had no use for him. Do you know what happened?"

"His family sued you for damaging their son?" I asked, half jokingly.

"No, we weren't nearly that litigious back then. After Jason's nose healed, he decided that he was smitten with me! My rejections just made him that much more determined, until he finally gave up and went after someone else."

"My mother, the heartbreaker *and* the nose breaker," I said.

"It wasn't my proudest moment, but there you go. Now, do we believe Megan?"

"I'm not sure," I said, though I liked her using the word "we."

"Then we put an asterisk by her name and move on to our next suspect. Is there anyone in particular you'd like to tackle first?"

"I was thinking we'd speak with Curtis and Wendy at the same time," I said. "Why not kill two birds with one stone?"

"An unfortunate expression, but that sounds like a solid enough plan to me."

"I still can't get over your story about breaking a boy's nose, and then he falls in love with you."

"It's all ancient history, Suzanne. Let's focus on the present, shall we?"

"We shall," I said with a grin.

CHAPTER 15

"**Y**ou're back," Wendy said the moment Momma and I walked into the office.

"We are indeed," I said. "Is your boss around?"

"He's at lunch," Wendy said as she stood. "If you'd like to make an appointment, I'd be glad to see if I can fit you in sometime next month." Wendy took a great deal of satisfaction in telling us that, but my smile never wavered.

"Actually, we'd love to talk to you instead," I said. "Right, Momma?"

"Absolutely. After all, you play a vital role here, Wendy, and we need your advice."

Momma sounded so sincere as she said it that I almost believed it myself. Wow, she was good.

"I'm not really all that important," Wendy said, suddenly blushing a little.

Score one for my mother! "On the contrary, you know the men you work for better than any of the other women in their lives probably do. After all, you spend more time with them and know just what they need to make them productive, what their strengths are, and more importantly, their weaknesses."

"I'll admit that it can be challenging with two of them, since sometimes they wanted two entirely different things, and it was always up to me to figure out what would be best for the both of them."

I kind of doubted that was even remotely true, but I wasn't

about to spoil my mother's good work. "Could you tell us a few things about what made Harley tick?" I asked.

"Oh, I couldn't divulge any company secrets," Wendy said quickly. "Mr. Daniels wouldn't like that."

Momma frowned at me for a moment, and then she said, "What my daughter means is, did he ask you to call him by his first name, or was everything formal around here?"

"Oh, he was friendly with me from the start," Wendy said. "It was never 'Mr. Boggess' with him, but always Harley."

"And Mr. Daniels? I notice you always use his last name when you speak of him."

"He likes things a little more formal," she conceded. "They were both great bosses, but in different ways."

"You say were. You're going to continue to work here for Mr. Daniels, aren't you?"

"He wants me to stay, no matter how he acts sometimes, but without Harley, I can't see myself hanging around. My sister's been trying to get me to move to Raleigh to be closer to her kids for years, and I've finally decided that's exactly what I'm going to do. Sooner rather than later, I'm going to take her up on her offer."

"So, you and Harley were really close then," I said.

"Sure, but not in a creepy kind of way or anything like that. He used to take time to give me advice, kind of take me under his wing, you know? He always said that the Christmas bonuses I got were from the firm, but I knew that if Mr. Daniels had any say in it, I'd get a card instead of a nice check every year."

"Was there generally a lot of tension between the two men?" I asked.

"No, Mr. Daniels claimed to be okay with giving me money, too. It was just Harley's idea, that's all."

I hadn't meant that. "I'm talking more about in general."

"Well, they were splitting up, but then you already knew that, didn't you?"

"We did," I said. "Would you have gone to work for Harley alone if he'd asked you to?"

"Well, I guess we'll never know that, will we," she said a little sadly.

"Why is that?"

"Because Harley never got the chance to ask," she said. Was there an air of wistfulness in her voice as she'd said that? I'd never thought of Harley Boggess as some kind of lady magnet, but apparently I'd been missing something. It was pretty clear that Wendy had been taken with him, too, just like Megan and Amber.

We were suddenly interrupted when the front door opened and Curtis Daniels came striding in. He was clearly surprised to see us there and just as obviously unhappy about our presence. "Seriously? Again? Unless you're here to do business with me, I've got work to do."

"We were just having a nice chat with Wendy," I said.

He wasn't pleased with that at all. "Oh, really."

"It was nothing confidential, Curtis," Momma said. "I bet you're going to miss her when she leaves the firm."

"So, she told you that, did she?"

"I didn't realize that it was supposed to be a secret," Wendy apologized to her remaining boss.

"Isn't it time for you to take your lunch?" he asked her icily.

"Yes, sir," she said, leaving the office without looking at either me or my mother on her way out.

"You were a little rough on her, weren't you?" Momma asked him after she was gone.

"I never wanted her here in the first place. She was Harley's hire, and I went along with it, but now that he's gone, I won't be needing her services any longer."

"I thought she just turned in her notice," I said, honestly confused now.

"She did, two minutes before I was about to fire her. She's working her last two weeks here, but if she keeps talking to strangers, she's not going to last even that long."

"We're hardly strangers," Momma said.

"It doesn't really matter at this point. She had a thing for Harley, can you believe that?"

"Why wouldn't she? He was handsome in his own way, and he could be quite charming when he wanted to be," Momma said.

"He never used any of that charm on me, I can tell you that. If I didn't know better, I'd say he brought her into the firm in the first place just to spy on me."

"Paranoid much?" I asked him.

"You're not being paranoid when someone really is out to get you," Curtis said. "I know for a fact that Harley was planning on forcing me to buy him out just so he could come after me once our company was dissolved."

"Didn't you have a noncompete clause in place to prevent that from happening?" Momma asked.

"Yes, but it was basically toothless."

"But that's not a problem for you anymore, is it?" I asked him, getting in a little jab.

"Believe me, for every problem that man's demise saved me, it created seven more to take its place," Curtis said. "I kept telling Harley that he was spending too much time on April Springs business and not enough time on ours, but he would never listen to me. Now that he's gone, I'm seeing just how right I was. I'll tell you one thing: I'm petrified about what the audit is going to show once it's been completed."

"You aren't accusing the dead man of stealing from you, are you?" Momma asked him.

"It's beginning to look as though it's not a question of if, it's a matter of how much," Curtis said. "It's a good thing I didn't know what he was up to. I might have done something drastic to the scoundrel myself."

"Like plunging a letter opener into his chest?" I asked him softly.

"What? Of course not. I would have done what any businessman worth his salt would do. I would have sued him for every penny he owed me, and then I would have seen him prosecuted to the fullest extent of the law."

"How much are we talking about here?" I asked.

"Over a hundred thousand dollars that I know of, and that's just so far," he said in disgust, and then he must have realized that he'd shared too much confidential information with us. "Why am I telling you two any of this? Dorothea, I'll ask you one last time: do we have any business to discuss, or are you two here on a witch hunt?"

"There's no business to be done anymore," she said simply. I might have tried to string him out a little, but so far, there was little to be critical of in my mother's performance.

"Then I'll ask you both to leave right now," Curtis said as he held the door open for us.

Momma and I had no choice but to go.

Once we were back in the car, I said, "You did a fine job in there."

"I don't know. I may have gotten more out of him if I'd dangled that deal in front of his nose, but I simply couldn't bring myself to do it."

"I totally get that," I said, "but look how much he told us. He practically gave us another motive for murder."

"And don't forget, Wendy isn't without blame, either. If she was spying on Curtis for Harley as Curtis claimed, it could have gone badly in the end."

"How so?" I asked.

"What if Harley asked Wendy to do more than she was comfortable doing? Harley had a big personality. Was it just me, or did Wendy seem a little too enthusiastic about her late boss?"

"She made him sound like Saint Harley," I conceded.

"I have a feeling that she was overcompensating for something. I'd love to know what their real relationship was like, in and out of the office. She has no real alibi for the time of the murder, remember."

"And no motive that we know of, either," I said. "That's crucial for us to make a case against her."

"Could he have spurned her affection as well?" Momma asked.

"I don't know. It's a stretch. I could see Megan falling for him, but Wendy seemed a bit more sensible than that."

"Then let's look for another motive. What if she was in on Harley's thefts, if indeed he even committed them in the first place?"

"I'm listening," I said. I loved the way my mother's mind worked, and hearing her think out loud was a real treat for me.

"She claimed that she knew a great deal of what was going on in this office. Let's take her at her word. Let's say she was snooping around, not only on Curtis but on Harley as well. She discovers Harley has been stealing from the company, and she demands a share for her silence. Harley decides she has to go, so he asks her to meet him in George's office so he can dispatch her without anyone being the wiser. The only thing was that Wendy's reactions were better than he thought they'd be, and she ended up striking out at him before he could do away with her. It's kind of like what happened with Phillip's old case. If you look at it that way, Wendy has no reason to stay now, since her hope of getting a cut of the proceeds is just as dead as Harley is."

"There are a great many 'what ifs' in that scenario," I said after mulling it over.

Momma looked crestfallen. "Sorry. I let my imagination run away with me."

"I'm not saying that it's not possible," I said. "The question is how do we prove it one way or the other?"

"We must continue as we've been doing and keep plugging away at it," Momma said. "Do we have time to interview one more suspect together, or do you need to speak to Amber with Grace?"

"Well, I've already spoken with Megan and Nathaniel this morning on my own, and we just talked to Curtis and Wendy. Would you mind terribly?"

"Not at all. I've got work to do myself," she said. "Could you drop me off at home?"

"I thought you drove to Donut Hearts this morning," I said.

"I was going to, but it was such a beautiful morning that I decided to walk. You know me. I like it when there's a bite in the air."

"I know you do." As I drove toward her home, I said, "Momma, it's really fun doing this with you."

Momma smiled in return. "Despite the grimness of the task, I think so, too. Perhaps next time, though, we do something more conventional, like see a play together or go shopping."

"You don't have to twist my arm," I said with a grin.

"It really is puzzling, isn't it?" she asked.

"I've seen worse cases, but not by much," I answered. "Harley had his fingers in quite a few pies, didn't he?"

"I dislike that expression, but in this case, I'll grant that it's apropos."

"I appreciate that."

We arrived at Momma's place, and as she was getting out of my Jeep, she said, "Happy hunting, Suzanne."

"Thanks."

I drove a few blocks and then pulled over before I called Grace. When she answered, I asked, "Hey, where are you?"

"I'm sitting in front of Amber North's house," she said.

"What? You weren't supposed to go there without me."

"I didn't. I was just driving by when I saw a strange car parked in front of her place. I pulled over and I was about to call you when my phone rang, and it was you."

"Don't move. I'll be there in two minutes." I could do it, too, if I didn't care about the speed limit or any of the other basic traffic laws.

I somehow made it in twenty seconds less than I'd predicted, but I couldn't find Grace when I got there.

Had something happened to her in the short time it had taken me to get there?

CHAPTER 16

"**G**RACE, WHERE ARE YOU?" I asked frantically the second she picked up when I called her back.

"I'm across the street," she said, "and a little down the block. Can't you see me waving at you? Keep driving past Amber's house and I'll get into your Jeep."

I did as she suggested, and after I parked out of sight, Grace came to the car on foot, grinning like a fool. "This is just like in the movies," she said as she got in.

"I can think of a dozen ways why it's nothing like it at all," I said.

"You don't consider skulking around in the shadows theatrical?"

"Well, for one thing, it's broad daylight, so I don't see any shadows. As to skulking, I wouldn't even know how to begin to do that."

"You know, like this," she said as she pretended to sneak around, holding her hands up like a squirrel's paws in front of her as she darted her head from side to side.

It was my turn to laugh. I couldn't help myself. She was hilarious. Getting myself under control, I asked her, "Did I miss anything on my way over here?"

"No, nobody's come out since I got here," she said. "Who do you think it might be, a secret boyfriend that Harley didn't know about and who maybe lashed out in a rage of jealousy at Harley for stealing Amber's attentions?"

What was it with the wild theories my investigative partners were spinning today? Was I becoming too staid in my approach to our crime-solving, or had they both suddenly decided to be overly dramatic at once? "I suppose it's possible," I conceded.

"But not probable; is that what you're saying?" Grace asked me as both of our gazes were riveted to Amber's front door.

"I'm not saying anything yet," I answered. While we waited on Amber's mysterious guest to come out, I brought Grace up to date on what Momma and I had uncovered.

"Wow, it sounds as though Wendy might have a motive after all," Grace said.

"Do you believe Momma's crazy theory?" I asked her.

"I know it sounds a little far-fetched, but in a certain light, it makes perfect sense. At least the theory matches the facts we have."

"In a twisted kind of way, I suppose," I said.

"Hey, at least it addresses our main concerns."

"It's too soon to say that yet," I said. "Is the door opening?" I glanced over and saw that Amber's front door was indeed beginning to open. Who was it? Could it indeed be a handsome, mysterious stranger coming to pay a call on her, or had I listened a little too intently to Grace's theory? The moment I saw that it was a woman, I knew that scenario had become even less likely, and when I finally saw who it was, I knew that there was something quite unusual about who was visiting Amber North.

What was Megan Gray, Amber's sworn enemy, doing visiting her in her home?

CHAPTER 17

I WAS OUT OF MY DOOR before I had a chance to tell Grace what I was doing. Truth be told, I didn't know myself at that moment. I just wanted to confront Megan and Amber together before they had a chance to get their stories straight.

"Megan, fancy finding you here," I said from afar, nearly out of breath in my rush to get to her before she had a chance to drive away.

She looked shocked to see Grace and me approaching. "Suzanne? Grace? Are you here to see Amber, too?"

"The real question is what are you doing here?" I said as I approached her. "After our talk this morning, this is the last place on earth I would have expected to find you."

"I came to clear the air," Megan said resolutely.

Amber was watching us from inside; at least the curtain fluttering said that much to me. What was she making of this? I'd have to ask her as soon as we moved on to her, but for now, Megan was in our sights.

"How did that work out for you?" Grace asked her.

"Not very well at all," Megan said, and then she threw her arms around me and started weeping.

"Take it easy," I said as I tried to disengage from her. Either this girl was on an emotional roller coaster, or she was trying to play on my sympathies yet again. Honestly, was this the only card she had in her deck? "We can't help you if you don't talk to us."

"Suzanne, she was just awful. I asked her for an apology, and she just laughed at me. Can you believe that?"

What I couldn't fathom was what had driven Megan there in the first place, if that had really been the purpose behind her visit. "It's unfortunate, but there's not much you can do about it," I said.

"I can't just stand out here like this," she said as she broke free and got into her car before we could stop her. She tried to speed away, nearly running Amber's mailbox down in the process.

I looked at Grace as Megan's car disappeared and asked, "What do we do now?"

"Do you believe her?" she asked me.

"I don't know. She's really convincing, isn't she?"

"All I can say is that if she's acting, she missed her calling. She's even better than Max."

"I wouldn't tell him that," I said as I started for Amber's front door.

I didn't even have to ring the bell before she opened it. "What did she just say about me? Did she tell you that I killed Harley?"

"No, his name never came up," I said, surprised that was where Amber had begun the conversation. "Why, did she accuse you of it just now?"

"Who knows what that fool was doing here? She started hinting around that I'd wronged her in some way and that the only way I'd ever find peace was if I begged her for forgiveness. Can you believe that? When I told her that she was barking up the wrong tree, she looked shocked that I wasn't playing by her script. I told Megan that I wasn't buying it and that she needed to get out before I threw her out. She looked outraged, but I was ready to do it. Harley didn't suffer fools gladly, and neither do I."

"Why did you bring up his name first?" Grace asked her from a step down off the porch.

"She clearly thinks I did it, the little nitwit. I ask you, why would I? Harley and I were going places. Someone killing him has ruined all of the careful work I put in on him."

"So what happens now, do you look for another councilman and start grooming him to oust George Morris? What do you have against the mayor, anyway?" I asked.

"Nothing except for the fact that he's a dinosaur. He wants to keep this town in the nineteen fifties, and I need to see some progress."

"You could always move someplace a little more to your taste," I suggested.

"April Springs is my home, and nobody's running me out." Amber took a step back, and then she had the satisfaction of slamming the door in our faces.

"That went well, didn't it?" I asked with a rueful smile.

"I can't imagine why she didn't apologize to Megan," Grace said.

We both laughed at that, and Amber came back out onto the porch. "Are you two laughing at me?" she asked us angrily.

"No, it was something Grace just said," I replied.

"About me?" She looked mad enough to come off the porch after us.

"Believe it or not, the entire world does not revolve around you, Amber," I said.

"You'd both better watch your steps," she said ominously.

"Is that a threat?"

"Take it any way you'd like to. I'm just saying, you've been warned."

Grace looked at her, fighting back a smile. "So noted."

Amber didn't know quite how to take that, so after a few moments, she went back inside, this time without the slam.

"We're in trouble now," Grace said the moment the door closed.

"Maybe we shouldn't have gone out of our way to anger a murder suspect," I said, the warning having a bit of a chilling effect on our conversation.

"Maybe not, but I refuse to tiptoe around, being careful not to offend anyone. April Springs might be her town, but it's ours as well," Grace said.

"Well said," I replied. "I'm afraid that we've just run out of suspects. What should we do now?"

Grace thought about it for a moment, and then she asked, "Would you feel good about asking Jake what kind of progress he's been making?"

"I don't know. Would you call Stephen?"

"Probably not. Well, unless we can find a new witness or a new piece of information, I'm not sure what we *can* do."

"Let's go somewhere and think about it," I said.

"Like the Boxcar?" Grace suggested.

"I don't know. I love Trish and her diner, but right now, I could use a breath of fresh air."

"We haven't been to Napoli's for a while," Grace suggested.

"That's true, and I'm always in the mood for Angelica's food. Sure, why not? Let's drop your car off at home, and I'll drive."

"It's a deal," she said. Our investigation might have stalled, but that didn't mean that we couldn't have something fantastic to eat, along with the best company outside of April Springs that I could ask for. Angelica and her daughters were just what I needed, a chance to be among friends and not focus solely on poor Harley Boggess's murder.

CHAPTER 18

UNFORTUNATELY, BY THE TIME WE got there, the parking lot was jammed, and there was a line of people outside waiting to get in.

"Should we go somewhere else?" Grace asked me.

"I kind of had my heart set on this," I said. "Why don't I drive around back?"

Grace grinned. "I love it. That way we can skip the crowd altogether."

"If they aren't too busy to feed us in the kitchen," I answered.

We knocked on the back door, and Maria, one of Angelica's beautiful daughters, opened up. She looked as frazzled as I'd ever seen her. "Is this a bad time?" I asked.

"No, of course not. Come on in. Momma's cooking."

We walked in, and Angelica's frown turned into a smile the moment she saw us. "Ladies, how nice to see you both."

"What's going on out there?" I asked her as I took off my coat. "Are you giving food away or something?"

"Practically," she replied, and then turned to her youngest daughter. "Sophia, would you care to tell them what happened?"

"I made a mistake, okay?" Sophia said. "I've already apologized like a dozen times, Mom."

"I wouldn't mind hearing it again," Antonia said. "I've got to get back out there. Wish me luck."

"Good luck," we all sang out, and Antonia smiled, despite the hungry crowd that was waiting for her.

"Sophia," her mother reminded her.

"I've been after Mom to try a newspaper ad to help fill some dead time in the afternoons between meals, so I placed a special between two and four this afternoon," she said.

"It appears that it was a success," I said with a grin.

"You don't know the half of it. The only problem was that the paper moved a decimal place on me. I ask you, Suzanne, how is that my fault?"

"Let me ask you something, Sophia. Did you read through the ad?" Angelica asked.

"I thought I did."

"Twice?" her mother asked.

"No, not twice."

"There you go. Instead of offering a taste of Italy for $14.95, we're offering it for $1.495. Where that half penny goes is beyond me."

"Can't you just post a notice and say that it was a mistake?" Grace asked her.

"Certainly," Angelica said with a smile. "Better yet, why don't you wade out there and tell them yourself?"

"No thanks," Grace said.

"No matter. We're making lots of pasta and sauce, and we're not turning anyone away. If you're here to allow me to feed you, you've both just made my day."

"Forget that," I said as I grabbed an apron. "If you are all in the kitchen, Antonia desperately needs help out front."

Grace grabbed one as well. "Do we need order pads?"

"Hardly," Maria said. "Everybody's getting the special today, which is not all that much of a surprise, is it?"

"That makes it easier," I said with a grin.

Angelica frowned. "I won't let you two work when you came here to eat."

"Angelica, what would happen if you came by Donut Hearts

and I was being overrun with customers? Would you demand a donut, or would you pitch in and help?"

"She's got you there, Mom," Sophia said with a grin.

"Really, Sophia? Do you choose to tease me right now?"

"Why not?" her daughter answered, still smiling. "After all, you can only kill me once."

Angelica's face softened. "I would never do that. You girls are my life." She then returned her gaze to us. "You ladies are a godsend," she said.

"Come on, Grace," I said with a smile, now that that was settled.

"Into the breach!" she shouted, and everyone started laughing.

Once we were in the dining room, the laughter stopped. Not only was every table full, but so was every seat. Antonia was working the room like a madwoman, and when she saw that we'd come to lend a hand, she smiled in relief.

"We're here to help. What can we do?"

She made no bones about accepting our assistance. "Grace, take the drinks. Suzanne, would you mind bussing the dirty tables?"

"I'd be happy to do it," I said. As we worked, Grace and I grinned at each other during those rare moments when we made eye contact. In a way, it was kind of fun, especially knowing that we were helping out friends in need. I stacked dirty dish after dirty dish and transported them into the kitchen, where the rest of the DeAngelis family worked in perfect harmony. As I ran the dishes through the dishwasher, I asked Angelica, "Are you going to lose much on this?"

"No, we should come close to breaking even, if we survive it," she said as she labored over two pots of boiling water. "The taste they're getting is heavy on the spaghetti, with a little lasagna and chicken Parmesan thrown in to round it all out."

"You know, this might work out in your favor after all," I said as I worked.

"How so?"

"You are getting a ton of good word of mouth from this. It looks like a publicity stunt that paid off instead of a mistake."

"Do you really think so, Suzanne?" Sophia asked as she mixed up another batch of fresh spaghetti.

"You never know," I said.

"See? I told you this would work," Sophia told her mother.

"We'll see," Angelica said, and then she winked at me.

Promptly at four, Angelica locked the front door, and Antonia stood by to let people out as they finished their meals. It was half an hour later before Grace and I got to eat in the kitchen with the rest of the DeAngelis women.

"That was kind of fun," Grace said as she finished eating.

"We couldn't have managed without you," Angelica said.

"You would have been fine, but thanks for letting us help out," I said as I stood. "What do we owe you for lunch?"

"One hug apiece will be sufficient," she said as the girls all swooped in on us to give us one giant family hug. Jake would have been envious if he'd seen it, as the DeAngelis matriarch was famous for raising beautiful daughters, and I couldn't blame him. After all, he was only human.

"Ladies, we owe you a debt of gratitude beyond words," Angelica said as she walked us out the back door.

"We were happy to help," I said.

"I promise you both that the next time you come, I won't make either one of you work," she said with a grin.

Once we were out of earshot of her daughters, I said, "Admit it, Angelica, you had fun."

"Of course I did," she said with a smile. "I'm the luckiest woman alive, working with my family at something I love doing. Safe journeys," she said as she added one last bonus hug for each of us.

Grace settled in beside me as we drove back to April Springs. "Wow, I don't know how they do that day in and day out. I just worked a few hours and I'm ready to drop. I can't imagine how you must feel, since you already put in a full shift at the donut shop."

"That was work," I said. "Napoli's was fun. I love that we were able to lend a hand."

"So do I, but we still haven't made much progress on our case."

"If it's all the same to you, I say we take it back up tomorrow after I close the donut shop for the day. I'm kind of beat myself."

"What are you and Jake going to have for dinner?" she asked.

"I'll make eggs for him," I said, "but I couldn't eat another bite. In fact, I'm going to go home, take a hot soak in the tub, and go to bed early tonight."

"I might do the same thing myself," she told me, and then we both started laughing. I loved having a best friend like Grace. She was always up for anything, and I knew that I could count on her, no matter what. We'd had fun, we'd helped a friend, and we'd still managed to eat some of the best food our area had to offer. I'd say that was a pretty good time, even if we hadn't advanced our case any.

Hopefully Jake had had more luck than we had.

"Let me get this straight. They all hugged you at once?" Jake asked later that night after I recounted my day's activities with him in front of the fireplace.

"I knew that would be the part you'd envy," I said with a grin. "Not that I blame you. It was a bit overwhelming being surrounded by that much beauty."

"I'm sure that you more than held your own," Jake said with a smile.

"Thank you, but we both know you're lying," I answered with a grin of my own.

"Suzanne, I wouldn't trade the whole clan for one of you, and that's the unvarnished truth," he said.

"You know what? I actually believe you."

"Why wouldn't you? I'm an officer of the law, committed to the truth, justice, and the American way."

"I thought that was Superman."

"It works just as well for me," he said, stretching out a little as he stifled a yawn. The poor thing was as beat as I was.

"Speaking of the law, did you make any more progress today than we managed to?"

"It's still hard to say," Jake replied. "You know how it goes. I plod along until I find something interesting that helps, but until then, I'm just gathering random facts."

"That is the biggest understatement about what you do that I've ever heard," I said. "You, sir, are a trained detective, outstanding in your field."

"You'd think so, wouldn't you? But if that were the case, why are small-town murders so much harder to solve than the cases I used to get when I was with the state police?"

"Could it be because back then, you didn't know any of your suspects? You'd come into a case with fresh eyes and see what didn't fit. Now that you're in one place all of the time, your thinking process has to be influenced by the fact that you know a great many of these people."

"You might be right," Jake said. "I don't think I gave Phillip enough credit when he had this job."

"Neither did I, but we can't tell him that now."

"Why not?"

"Jake, I'm not sure the man's ego could handle it. He's just now settling into someone I don't mind being around. If we puff him up any, he might go back to his old ways."

"You like him, don't you?"

"I'm beginning to," I admitted, "but if you tell him I said that, I'll just deny it."

Jake laughed as it was my turn to yawn. "You look beat. Shouldn't you be off to get some sleep?"

"I need to, but I hate leaving you out here all alone."

"Don't worry about me. I'll be there soon enough."

After he kissed me good night, I decided that I'd give it five minutes. If he didn't make it in by then, I'd get up and rejoin him out on the couch, no matter how much my body might protest the move.

The only problem was that I was asleep before my head hit the pillow.

I woke up more on instinct than anything else, watching my alarm go off just as I opened my eyes.

The bed beside me was empty, though. Had Jake already left, even given the hour?

He was still on the couch, snoring softly. The poor dear hadn't even made it to the bedroom. I covered him with a throw, kissed his forehead, and then left for work. I had a busy day ahead of me between Donut Hearts and my investigation, and I knew that I had to get cracking. I just didn't realize how sore I'd be after basically pulling two shifts yesterday, one at the donut shop and the other at Napoli's. I couldn't do that very often, but I was still happy that Grace and I had pitched in.

As I drove down the short section of Springs Drive between the cottage I shared with Jake and Donut Hearts, I marveled about how many good friends I'd accumulated over the years. I wasn't rich in terms of my finances, and Jake and I would be working until we were old and gray based on what we currently made, but I wouldn't have traded my life for that of the richest person in the world, not if it meant giving up the people I knew and loved. It was being wealthy in a way that meant more to me than any bank account, and I felt blessed just to be able to live the life I led.

As I walked into the donut shop, flipping on lights and the fryer in the kitchen, I started on the donuts for another day. Emma wouldn't be in for a while, and as I settled into my morning solitary routine, I let part of my mind wonder about why someone had murdered Harley Boggess. We'd certainly found enough folks that had their reasons, at least in their own minds. Sorting them out to find the guilty one was the problem. I wished that I had some litmus test to use, but if there was anything in this case that might act as one, I didn't know what it might be. As always, the motive had to be the key. Either Curtis or Wendy could have done it because of greed, Nathaniel could have been motivated by power, while Amber and Megan could have done it because of their hearts. Who would have guessed that there would be so many reasons to kill the man? As I worked on the cake donuts, I decided that we needed more information before we tackled our suspects again. I had a feeling that we'd gotten as much as we could out of them based on questioning alone.

It was time to sniff around the edges of Harley's life to see if there was something that Jake and everyone else had been missing.

I just wasn't sure how to go about it, at least not yet, but I had faith in my group. After all, we'd managed to find killers before. That confidence made me believe that we could do it this time as well.

CHAPTER 19

"D o you have any of them raspberry-filled donuts?" a young girl asked me as she looked over my donut stock a few hours after we'd opened for the day. She was too young to be in grade school, and apparently her mother had brought her into the shop just to get her out of the house. After a bit, I understood why she might crave some adult contact, but I didn't know it at that moment. What was odd was that they hadn't approached the counter together; instead, the mother hovered nearby, no doubt trying to give her daughter a little sense of independence.

"Sorry, we didn't make any of those today. We have lemon filled," I offered.

"How about strawberry?" she asked with a frown.

"There's cherry. Is that close enough?"

"No," she said. After frowning at the case again, she turned to her mother. "They don't have no raspberry, or no strawberry, either," she said. "This place stinks. Can we go somewhere else?"

The little lady's charm had suddenly worn off on me. "Let me know when you decide," I said as I wiped down the counter.

"Heather, just pick one," her mother said as she approached us, and then, as an aside to me, she added, "Sorry about that. Heather always has been precocious."

"No worries," I said, though I could think of a few other words that might describe her more aptly. "I'm just sorry she caught me on a day where raspberry and strawberry were both off the menu. I like to rotate my filled donuts so my customers don't get bored with my offerings. How about custard?"

"Where are the Santa donuts?" the little girl asked me with a deepening frown.

"We stop selling those after Christmas," I explained.

"Why would you do that?" she asked pointedly.

"Well, Santa needs his rest after what he's been through."

Her lip curled a little. "I don't care anymore. Just give me a plain one."

"It would be my pleasure," I said as I grabbed her a plain old-fashioned cake donut and put it on a plate.

"Not that kind," she said, nearly wailing about my incompetence. "The kind with icing on it."

"You want a raised donut, then," I said, swapping out the cake for a yeast one. "Would you care for anything to drink?"

"Do you have Kool-Aid?" she asked me.

"No, but we have some nice hot cocoa you might like."

"Forget it," she said as she shoved a handful of sticky change toward me. The reason I knew that it was sticky was because it clung to the counter as though it had been coated with glue. That would have probably been preferable to what it was really covered in.

"Isn't she such a fine little lady? She earned that money herself by picking up her toys without having to be asked more than three times," Heather's mother explained as her daughter inhaled the donut I'd just put before her.

"How nice," I said.

"Do I get any change back?" the little pain demanded.

I looked down at the money and saw that she was actually eleven cents short, but I wasn't about to tell the little princess that. "No, we're good."

After her donut was gone, Heather looked at her mother. "I thought it would be better than that. Can we go now?"

At least her mom had the decency to usher her out of there before I had a complete meltdown. I understood that the little girl was just a child, but had manners gone completely out of fashion? I felt like Grandma Hart as I took a clean dishtowel and gathered the change up as best I could. Emma came out of the kitchen with a grin on her face.

"Did you hear that?" I asked.

"I did," she said. "Wow, I can't believe how well you handled her."

"What can I say? I'm a people person. Here," I said as I thrust the towel at her. "Why don't you clean this money, and then we can put it in the till."

Emma opened the towel and looked inside. "This is disgusting," she said.

"Tell me about it. I'm not sure that counter will ever get clean enough for me again." I got out some strong cleaner and went to work on it, and soon enough, it was back to its pristine condition, though every time I glanced at that spot, I saw the goo-covered coins there in my mind.

The rest of my morning was fairly uneventful. We had a steady stream of customers come by, but none of our suspects made an appearance, and really, why would they? None of our last conversations had gone all that well, and I couldn't imagine any of them seeking me out for more of the same. What I needed was a new source of information, and there was only one untapped one I could think of. After I closed Donut Hearts for the day, I was going to have to go pay a visit to Gabby Williams.

It turned out that I didn't have to do that after all. Twenty minutes before closing time, she came to me instead.

"Suzanne, why haven't I seen you lately?"

"Hello, Gabby. As a matter of fact, I came by to see you earlier, but you were closed."

"What can I say? I felt like getting out of town," she said. "Sometimes a drive can do wonders. What were you trying to see me about?"

She knew the purpose of my visit, and what's more, I knew that she knew that I'd been coming to her for information about Harley Boggess. I suddenly got very stubborn at the thought that she was holding it over me now, and I vowed not to ask her for help if the case's solution itself depended on it. "I wanted to see if you had any new blouses in that fit me. Jake's been talking about taking me to Charlotte for a night out next weekend."

"Sorry, I'm not sure I have anything in your size that would look good on you," she said almost automatically.

If she was expecting to get a rise out of me, I planned to disappoint her. "Thanks for coming by, then. You just saved me a trip."

She looked flustered at my cavalier handling of her rebuff, and it was clear that Gabby didn't know quite what to do next.

"May I interest you in any donuts?" I asked as sweetly as I could manage.

"No, you know I don't care for them any more, not since that incident we had." Gabby had experienced a bad encounter with a customer with a grudge once who'd peppered her place with pastry, and she'd never forgiven me for selling them to him in the first place.

"Then you have yourself a nice day," I said, and then I just stood there, smiling at her like an idiot.

She had no choice, really; Gabby decided to leave before things got even more confusing. I relished my small victory for a moment, and then I realized that I'd only punished myself by my mischievous behavior. Gabby could have witnessed the murder herself, but she wouldn't tell me about it now. I'd have to find a way to apologize for my rashness and try to get on her good side again, if I'd ever in fact been on it in the first place.

I heard from Grace ten minutes before I was due to close. "Suzanne, I'm going to be late," she said.

"Problems at work?"

"I suppose you could say that. No good deed goes unpunished, you know?"

"What do you mean?"

"My rep with the excess suitors included me in her problem," Grace said. "It turns out that the one she ended up rejecting wants my head on a platter, and I've got to go calm him down before he does something stupid."

"Would you like me to go with you?" I asked. "It might not be safe for you to see him alone."

"I've already thought of that. Jake is giving Stephen enough time off to go with me. Ordinarily I'd handle this on my own, but I've got a cop for a boyfriend, so why wouldn't I use his help if he offered it?"

"I think you'd be foolish to turn him down," I said. "Let me know how it goes."

"I will, but it might be a while," she said.

"That's fine. Momma and I will carry on without you as best we can."

"That's what I'm afraid of. I hate missing all of the action."

"Grace, at this point, I don't think there's any action to miss. See you later."

"I'll call you when I get back home," she said. I hoped that this experience didn't put Grace off helping others. Of the two of us, I was the busybody of the pair. I couldn't help myself. If

I saw someone going astray, how could I not say something? Come to think of it, that was one of my biggest complaints with my mother, butting in where her advice hadn't been sought in the first place. I didn't care to think about how far my apple had fallen from her tree, so I set about getting ready to close up shop for the day.

Momma came in just as I finished my deposit slip and zipped the bag shut. Emma had already headed out, since she had an early class to catch. As for me, I was ready for some action.

"Suzanne, I'm afraid I won't be able to join you this afternoon in your sleuthing," she said.

"What do you mean? You're right here," I said.

"Alas, not for long. I have a meeting I cannot avoid any longer. If things work out in my favor, which I'm going to do my utmost to ensure happens, I could make a substantial profit from the deal."

"Momma, why do you work so hard? You're already so rich you couldn't spend it all in three lifetimes, and if you're worrying about leaving anything to me, I'm pretty happy with the way things are right now."

"Suzanne, I don't do it for the money. It's fun," she said.

"If you say so. I'd rather make donuts myself."

"Then we're both perfectly suited for our chosen occupations. Surely Grace will be more than happy to fill in for me."

"I'm sure she will," I said, not wanting to share with Momma that our third partner was absent as well. If she knew that Grace was someplace else, she'd worry about me, and I wasn't too keen on that happening.

She must have read some subtle clue in my voice or my expression though, because she picked right up on it. "Suzanne, Grace is coming, isn't she?"

"After a brief delay, she'll be here," I admitted. Lying to her was not an option.

"I could always cancel my meeting," Momma said as she reached for her cellphone.

"Don't you dare," I said. "Contrary to popular belief, I don't need a babysitter around the clock."

"I didn't mean to imply that you did," Momma said calmly. "I just don't think it's safe for any of us to work alone on this."

"I won't," I said, knowing that it was the truth. As crazy as it sounded, if I went against what I'd just promised my mother, I'd never be able to forgive myself, even if I ended up dying because of it.

"Good. Be patient, and the answers you seek will come to you."

"Now you sound like a bad fortune cookie," I said with a grin.

"My opinion is always that any fortune cookie is better than no fortune cookie at all," she said with a smile. "I'll touch base with you later."

"Good luck with your meeting."

"My dear, sweet child, I can assure you that luck has nothing to do with it."

After I drove my deposit to the bank, I had no idea what to do next. Maybe if I drove around town, an idea would spark and I'd know where to go next once I had reinforcements. There were four activities I generally used to come up with new ideas: a walk, a drive, a shower, and a nap. Okay, the nap rarely worked, but hey, even if it didn't, I'd still get a nap. I drove around a bit before I resorted to one of my other options when I found myself in front of Nathan's Sport Shop. It wasn't a place I ordinarily visited, but I remembered that I wanted another softball bat for the donut shop, so I pulled into the parking lot and went in. The owner himself was there, all dressed in camouflage and looking as though he were ready to go hunting, which he may have been, for all I knew. I didn't participate in that particular activity, so I wouldn't know.

"Suzanne Hart, as I live and breathe," Nathan said. "Or is it Bishop these days?"

"No, it's still Hart," I said.

"I should have pegged you for one of those modern women."

I was about to unload on him with both barrels when I noticed that he was smiling at me. "You picked a bad day to poke the bear, Nathan. I almost came after you."

"Don't think I didn't just see it in your eyes. Wow, you must be having one supremely bad day. Sorry about that crack. You know I didn't mean anything by it."

"Before you had Evie, I might not be so sure, but I know how much having that daughter of yours has turned you into a big softy."

"Hey, keep it down, will you? You'll ruin my rep around here," he said with a grin.

"Do you have any new pictures on you?"

"I might be able to find one or two," he said, his smile broadening as he pulled out his phone and brought up the latest crop of shots.

"She's adorable, isn't she?"

"You'd have to ask someone else. I'm prejudiced."

"As well you should be," I said.

"I know you didn't come by to look at baby pictures, Suzanne. What can I do for you?"

"I'm looking for a softball bat," I said.

As we walked to the sporting goods section of his shop, he asked, "What happened, did you lose the last one you bought from me?"

"No, but I'd feel better having two at the shop."

He shook his head. "Suzanne, you need something a little more powerful than that for protection."

"I'm married to the chief of police, Nathan. How much more protection do you think I need?" I asked him.

"Maybe more than this," he said as he handed me the bat. There was a look in his eyes that I didn't like.

"Nathan, what aren't you telling me?"

"It's probably nothing," he said. "Don't worry about it."

"Now I'm really concerned," I answered. "Come on. Talk."

"You and Grace are looking into Harley Boggess's murder, aren't you?"

"It's not that big a secret around town," I conceded. "Why do you ask?"

"It might be nothing, but I heard from a friend of a friend of a friend that you were butting in a little too much, and you'd better watch your step."

"Well, with a source as unimpeachable as that, how can I not listen?" I asked.

"You need to take this seriously. I haven't been able to find out who said it originally, but the word on the street is that if you don't back off, you're going to regret it."

"You know what? That's the best news I've had all day," I said as I walked to the cash register with my new bat.

"Suzanne, did you hear me just now? This is no joke."

"I certainly hope not," I said.

"Then why are you so happy about it?" The poor man was clearly confused by my reaction to his news.

"If someone cares enough to threaten me, then I must be getting to them," I said.

"Let me get this straight. You're happy about making a killer angry with you?"

"Let's just say that it's the only way I can measure my progress at this point. How much do I owe you for the bat?"

"Let's see, after the courtesy discount, it comes to seventeen dollars and thirty-six cents."

As I handed him a twenty, I asked, "What's the courtesy discount for?"

"You asked to see a photo of my daughter," he said softly as he winked at me. "I've been doing it for a while, and nobody's caught me at it yet. When other folks start demanding a discount as well, I'll probably stop doing it, but for now, I'm having a little fun with it."

After I got my change, I thanked Nathan and headed back out to my Jeep, carrying my new purchase over my shoulder like a big-league ball player. At least I thought that's the way I was toting it, but I didn't really know how a major leaguer would carry it, so I could have been dead wrong. All I knew was that it felt good having it on my shoulder, and if the time ever came that I had to use it to defend myself, I hoped that I'd be able to do it without hesitation.

CHAPTER 20

I DIDN'T FEEL LIKE GOING BACK into Donut Hearts to drop off the bat, so I stowed it beside my seat for the moment. I was still no better off than I had been before. Even if I'd managed to enrage the killer, I still didn't know who it was, so I was just as lost as I had been before. I needed to take action, and it was killing me that I had to wait for someone to go with me. Maybe if I just phoned one of my suspects, it wouldn't count as an interrogation. I discarded the idea as quickly as I'd gotten it. I needed to see people's reactions to the things I said, and that was something that I just couldn't do over the phone. I was still trying to figure out what to do when Seth Lancaster tapped on my windshield. "Are you okay, Suzanne?" he asked me.

"I'm fine. I was just lost in my thoughts for a second there," I said. "How are you, Seth?"

"Physically, I'm fine and dandy. Financially, well, that's a whole other story."

"Is the market hitting you hard? I heard that Nathaniel Bloom was a good advisor."

"To give him credit, he probably is. I know it's a bad time to be playing the stock market. I can read a newspaper as well as anyone else can, but if he can't do better than he's doing, I'm going to have to find somebody else." Seth laughed a little, and then he added, "Not that I didn't make him jump through some hoops the morning I had my appointment with him."

"Did your meeting last long after Grace and I left?" I asked him.

"It wasn't so much that as it was the times before it," he said.

"What do you mean?"

"I spent most of the morning on the phone with Nathaniel changing my mind about what strategy I wanted to use for my investing. I've got to give him credit. He did a week's worth of work in one morning, especially when I kept throwing him so many curveballs. If he left his desk long enough to go the bathroom all morning, it would have surprised me."

"Are you sure about that?" I asked him.

"Well, I suppose he could have ducked out for thirty seconds, but I doubt it was a minute longer. I must have called him a dozen times, and I have to give the man credit. He picked up on the first ring every time."

"Did you call his cellphone number or his office?" I asked. That could be a vital piece of information.

"I don't have the man's cellphone number. He's too smart to give me that. It was the office, every time. Why do you ask?"

"Did he ever sound out of breath, or shaken a little when you spoke?" I asked.

"No, I expected him to get frazzled a time or two, but he answered every time just as calm and patient as always. I don't know how he works with that opera music in the background, but I heard it playing every time I called. That would drive me nuts if I had to listen to that stuff all day, but to each his own. Say, why all the questions?"

"Can't I just be curious by nature?" I asked him with a smile.

"That's a woman's prerogative, isn't it?" he asked, grinning in return.

"And a man's, as well," I said with a laugh.

"Isn't that the truth? Women get a bad rap for being gossips, but men are a dozen times worse, if you ask me. As a matter of fact, I'm doing it right now, aren't I? See you at the donut shop soon, Suzanne."

"I'll be there," I said. "Thanks."

"For what, I don't know, but I'll accept anyway."

After he was gone, I mulled over what he'd just told me. If what Seth had said was accurate, and I had no reason to believe that it hadn't been, Nathaniel had been telling me the truth. He didn't have time between phone calls to go to City Hall, kill Harley, and make it back to his office in time for his next phone call. Knowing that Seth could be calling again any second would have kept him chained to his desk just as effectively as if he'd literally been tethered in place. The use of his office phone, with his music playing constantly in the background, sealed that as well. Unless we learned something else that contradicted what I'd just learned, Nathaniel had just made it off of our list of suspects.

One done and four to go.

Something kept nagging me. We had reasonable motives for murder for the last four folks on our list, with one glaring exception. Curtis stood to inherit Harley's half of the business without any cost to him, so that had to make him a viable suspect. If Momma's theory that Wendy had been blackmailing Harley and it had gone bad was true, she had reasons of her own, and if Megan had killed him for humiliating her, I could see that as well. But why would Amber do it? Could Harley have been leaving her, and she couldn't take the rejection? No, Amber seemed the type of woman who would just write him off as a lost cause and move on to the next man. What possible reason would she have to kill him? I didn't know, but I wanted to find out. The only problem was that I didn't have a partner to go brace her with, and I'd promised Momma that I wouldn't do it alone. Did that mean that I had to use one of them, though? I'd had another partner once upon a time before he'd first run for mayor. No one could object if George went with me, and if anyone had a stake in solving this murder, it was him. After all, suspicion would hover over him like a dark cloud until this murder was solved and he was proven innocent. Ordinarily I didn't like to include our mayor in my investigations, but he was already all the way up to his eyebrows in this one. I considered calling him, but after a moment's thought, I decided to see him in person, as much as it troubled me to return to the crime scene.

"George, do you have a minute?" I asked the mayor as I entered his office. I was surprised to see a card table and a folding chair where his former desk and chair had so recently been.

"Suzanne, it's nice to see you," he said from the window. "You're about the only person brave enough to visit me right now."

"How bad is it?" I asked.

"Pretty bad." He gestured to his new arrangements. "What do you think?"

"What happened? Did Jake confiscate your office furniture?"

"The chair was ruined, but I didn't want the desk anymore, either. It was just a reminder of what happened. Suzanne, somebody tried to set me up to take the fall for murder, and the more I think about it, the angrier I get."

"I completely understand that," I said. "Would you like to do something about it?"

"Just point me in the right direction," he said eagerly.

"I could use a backup when I go talk to Amber North," I said.

He smiled. "I thought you were finished with me as a partner. Since I got hit by that car, you've shied away from using me."

Once, long ago, George had been dealing with a killer on my behalf, and to keep from being captured, she'd run him down with her car. He'd mostly recovered from the attack, but on chilly days he sometimes still walked with a slight limp, a reminder of how close he'd come to getting killed doing something for me. "What can I say? If anyone has a right to be involved in this, it's you."

"Let's go," he said.

"Don't you have to tell anyone first?" I asked him.

He laughed as he looked around the empty corridor outside his office. "Exactly who would you like me to tell?"

"Okay then, let's go."

We walked out and got into my Jeep. After George was buckled in, he reached down and picked up the aluminum bat I'd bought from Nathan earlier. "Are you going out for the softball team?" he asked me with a grin.

"It's protection for the store," I said.

"Well, if you're going to keep carrying it around in your Jeep, take my advice and throw in an old ball and glove, too."

"George, you do understand that I'm not going to actually use it to play softball, right?"

"Maybe not, but a bat alone can be considered a weapon, and it can get you into trouble if you're ever pulled over. Throw in a ball and a glove though, and you have reasonable doubt."

"It's probably not a bad idea," I said, "but I'm not planning on keeping it in my Jeep past tomorrow morning."

"I'm just saying," George said, and then he trailed off.

Once we got to Amber's place, the mayor was raring to go. "How should we play this, good cop/bad cop? If we are, I've had some practice playing the bad cop."

"Why am I not surprised?" I asked him with a smile.

"What is that supposed to mean?"

"I know you and love you, but you still sometimes scare me," I said.

"Me? Scary? I don't believe it," he said happily. I had a hunch that I'd just made his day. I could live to be a thousand and I still wouldn't understand what passed as a compliment to men. Then again, I was sure that women were just as cryptic to them about a host of other topics. As far as I was concerned, that was what made life so interesting.

"Let's just probe her a little about her relationship with Harley and see where that leads us," I suggested.

"Fine. It's your investigation," he said. "I'm just happy to be able to do something instead of sitting back and waiting for something to happen."

On the drive over, I brought George up to speed on what we'd learned about Amber so far, confining my explanation to only her and not the slew of other suspects we had. I didn't want George off his focus. I needed him to be centered on only one suspect at a time.

I knocked on Amber's door a few times, and I was starting to believe that she wasn't home when George took over. My knock had been a request; his pounding was a demand. It said, "Open the door, or we're going to break it down."

"What is it?" Amber said, clearly aggravated until she saw that the mayor was with me. It was pretty clear that if it had been me and Grace or even Momma, she wouldn't have answered a single question. Somehow, purely by accident, I'd found the perfect partner for this particular situation. "Mayor, what are you doing here?"

"We need to talk, Amber," George said, slipping so easily back into his role as a cop that it startled me, and I'd been expecting it.

"What about?" she asked warily.

"What do you think? Are you going to invite us in, or do you want to do this out here in front of anybody who happens to be driving by?"

It was an effective tactic. Amber looked up and down the road, and then she stepped aside. "You might as well come in."

We did as we were instructed, but instead of addressing us, she walked over to the coffee table in front of the television, picked up the remote control, and started hitting buttons. "If I don't tape this now, I'll forget all about it."

It was a wonder this woman ever did a lick of work, and if she'd had to pay her cable bill by the hour, she would have had to take out a second mortgage on the house.

"Tell us about Harley," I said once we had her attention again.

"What about him? I'm sure the two of you knew him longer than I did."

"But not as intimately," I said. I'd chosen that word carefully to see if I could get a reaction from her, but it failed.

"Harley wasn't exactly a complex man, you know? He didn't have enough ambition to suit me, but I knew that if I worked with him, he'd eventually come around."

"So you wanted to start by helping him take my job away from me, is that it?" George asked her.

It was a little stronger than I would have gone, but I couldn't do anything about that.

Amber said, "No offense, but Harley was meant for bigger and better things. He wasn't going to stop at your office. I had big plans for him before he was murdered."

"How did he feel about your aspirations?" I asked her.

"What do you mean?"

"Your plans for his career," George explained.

She looked at him as though he were an idiot. "I know what the word means, Mr. Mayor," she said with a tone of derision in her voice.

"Then answer the question," George said, nonplussed by her rebuff. "Did he share your goals, or did the two of you fight about it?"

"We never argued," Amber said.

"Really? Never? That's not what I heard," I said.

"Sure, we had some heated discussions, but it never amounted to anything. Before he died, Harley was as excited about his prospects as I was."

"So, according to you, you had a perfect relationship," I said, making sure that I expressed plenty of doubt in the statement.

Amber just laughed. "Perfect? Hardly. He wasn't the easiest man in the world to get along with, but then again, I don't think any of them are picnics, you included, Mr. Mayor."

"George is fine," the mayor said, no doubt getting tired of hearing the sarcasm in her voice every time she used the title. "Let's talk about this alibi of yours," he said.

"That's right. I've been meaning to tell you about that, Suzanne," she said, crowing a little as she spoke. "It turns out that I've got one after all."

"How's that?" I asked.

"I forgot all about something that happened that morning that clears me of suspicion."

"I can't wait to hear this," I said.

"You can be as skeptical as you'd like, but you can call her and see that I'm telling the truth. That should get you off my back once and for all."

"Who exactly are we supposed to call?" George asked.

"Effie Robbins," she said.

"What about Effie?" She'd been a customer at my shop on occasion, a pretty girl who'd just graduated from high school with not many prospects. Effie was a literal kind of gal, not the brightest bulb in the chandelier by any stretch of the imagination and a difficult one to hold a conversation with.

"She was at my house all morning," Amber said. "She was upstairs the entire time, and I forgot all about her even being there until after you left my place."

"How could you have forgotten her?" I asked.

"I let her in, along with some other women, and then I

started watching my shows. You know how I get. A bomb could go off under my chair and I wouldn't notice."

The woman was obsessed with her television, that much I could testify to myself.

"Why was she in your house in the first place?" George asked.

"She was trying out for a job with my cleaning company," Amber said.

"All morning?" I asked.

"Well, the fact is that I found her upstairs asleep in my bed. She had cleaned about half of it, and then she'd crawled in for a four-hour nap. It turned out that she went dancing the night before her interview until all hours. Three girls came and cleaned, and I just assumed that Effie left with them. I don't know, I was watching something. I went up to take a nap myself after you left and I found her passed out in my bed."

"Did she get the job?" I asked with a grin.

"What do you think? Anyway, I'm covered," she said smugly.

"As soon as we confirm it," George said.

"She'll tell you the truth," Amber said as she glanced back at her television.

"Even if you're telling the truth, why couldn't you have just slipped out, killed Harley, and then come back home without Effie even knowing that you were gone?"

"The door to my bedroom squeaks like a banshee, and if I went in there to get my car keys, I would have woken her up when I went in, not to mention spotting her snoozing in my bed. Now, was there anything else, or can I get back to my life?"

"Did Megan really come by last night to apologize?" I asked her as she ushered us out of her home.

"Who knows? She tried to say something, but honestly, I don't trust that girl as far as I can throw her."

"Megan? She wouldn't hurt a fly, would she?" George asked.

Leave it to the mayor to expect the best out of people. Then again, I hadn't told him that she was one of our suspects.

"When I told her she was being ridiculous, she got all cold on me, you know?" Amber asked as she shivered a little. "I might have been a little crazy making fun of her."

"Why, because you're feeling remorse?" I asked.

"No, because now I have to watch my back. If she killed Harley for laughing at her, what's to keep her from coming after me next?"

"What? Do you honestly think she could have done it?" George asked incredulously.

"We'll talk about it later," I told him.

"Talk about it anywhere you'd like to, but just not here," Amber said.

Once we were out on the porch, George said, "Maybe you should bring me up to speed on all of your suspects."

"Are you sure that's a good idea?" I asked him.

"Suzanne, you said it yourself. Until this case gets solved, my prospects for reelection are somewhere between slim and none, not to mention my freedom for the rest of my life. What choice do I have?"

I knew that he was right, but all of a sudden, I had a team of coworkers trying to help me solve Harley's murder. It would be a wonder if we didn't all end up tripping over each other, but who could I say no to, my best friend, my mother, or the man who was being impacted most by what had happened? Like it or not, I had more help than I needed, or even wanted, for that matter.

Maybe it would make my job easier.

I doubted it, but it was nice to think that it might be so.

CHAPTER 21

"WELL, IT'S TRUE," I SAID after I called Effie and got her side of the story. "She was there all morning."

"So Amber's in the clear," George said.

"Her alibi might not be airtight, but it's going to have to do for now. We can keep her in the back of our minds, but for the moment, let's draw a line through her name."

"What other names do you have on your list?" George asked me.

In for a dime, in for a dollar, I thought. "We have three suspects left: Curtis Daniels, Wendy Crouch, and Megan Gray."

"Motives?" George asked, going into full cop mode. Did they ever lose that, even after they'd been off the job for over a dozen years?

"Curtis out of greed, Wendy to protect herself, and Megan from the anger of being rejected."

"Explain more," he commanded. After I went into a little more detail about each suspect, he asked, "Do you have alibis for any of them?"

"Actually, we have one for each of them, no matter how shaky they might be," I said.

"You've been busy," he said with some admiration.

"What can I say? It's been a process."

After I told George the sketchy alibis we had, he frowned. "There's not much to go on there, is there?"

"Hey, things are a great deal better than they were earlier today."

"That's right, you've taken Amber North off of your list."

"And Nathaniel Bloom, as well," I told him, and then I shared Nathaniel's alibi with him.

"Makes sense. So we have three suspects and four detectives working the case."

"Not including Jake," I said.

"That's what I meant. Should we work in one big group, or should we break up into teams?" he asked me.

I was still trying to find an answer for that when Grace called me. "Suzanne, where are you? I'm with your mother, so you'd better not be investigating without us."

"Actually, George is with me," I said. "I have news. Where should we meet?"

"I'm starving. Let's go to the Boxcar," Grace said.

I turned to George. "Are you hungry?"

"I could eat," he said with a shrug.

"The Boxcar it is," I said.

When George and I got there, Trish was standing at the door grinning at me. "The other members of your party have already arrived."

"Thanks."

"Aren't you going to invite me over, too?" she asked impishly.

"Before this is over, you'll probably get a handwritten invitation yourself," I said with a sigh.

"Oh, goody. You know how much I love a party. I'll be right there with the menus, unless you two want the special, too. Today we're serving turkey, mashed potatoes and gravy, green beans, and cranberry sauce."

Jessica Beck

"It's not Thanksgiving again already, is it?" George asked with a smile.

"What can I say? I was in the mood for a little holiday meal. Where is it written that we can only have it on a special day?"

"The special sounds good to me," I said, and George nodded in assent.

"Excellent. I'll have them out for you soon, along with a pair of sweet teas."

After everyone said their hellos, I brought the group up to speed as to what I'd been up to. Everyone had a ton of questions, and I was still talking by the time the food arrived. At least the diner wasn't very crowded, so we didn't have to worry about too many eavesdroppers listening in.

"Go on," George said after Trish had delivered our food. Everything looked wonderful, and she'd even added a bit of stuffing to the side of my plate, though she hadn't mentioned it earlier. I'd managed to hide my disappointment at its exclusion, so I was happy to see it now.

"May I eat first?" I asked as my mouth began to water.

"We can fill in for you from here," Grace said, "but I have an idea. Let's table the crime discussion and give this meal the attention it deserves. Any seconds of my motion?"

Were we so large now that we were using parliamentary procedure to get through a meal? I was about to object when my own mother said, "Seconded."

Grace said, "All in favor, say aye."

There was a consensus, but she asked for opposing votes just to make it official, and we dove into our meals without a single reference to what had brought us all there together.

Maybe the idea hadn't been so bad after all. At least I got to eat without being interrupted, so that was something.

After we finished, I said, "I know we need to talk, but this isn't the best place to do it. Should we adjourn to Donut Hearts?"

"Aren't you afraid people will think that you're open?" Grace asked.

"I'm willing to risk it this once," I said as I noticed that the diner was beginning to fill up.

"Then let's go," Momma said.

"Shouldn't we put it to a vote first?" Grace asked with a smile.

"No thanks," I said. "This is a benevolent dictatorship, not a democracy. Are there any objections to that? Somebody needs to lead this team of maniacs, and unless one of you has a better idea, it's going to be me."

When no one spoke, I smiled softly. "Good. The motion is carried. Now let's go."

Momma picked up the entire check, leaving a generous tip as well, much to our protests. It was all in vain though, as my arguments with my mother normally were, and soon enough we were seated in the front of my donut shop, with everyone looking expectantly at me.

I'd asserted my authority earlier, and now I had to back it up.

I just wished that I knew what our next best step was.

"The best place to start is to figure out where we are right now," I said.

"You just caught me up on everything, Suzanne," George protested.

"Now, George, be patient with her," Momma said.

"You don't have to defend me, Momma," I said.

"I was only trying to help," she replied.

"I know you were, and I appreciate it."

"I wouldn't mind hearing it again," Grace said. "Maybe it will jar something loose in my mind."

I silently thanked her with a smile, which she returned in full. I continued, "We know that Curtis, Wendy, and Megan each had possible reasons to want to see harm come to Harley. The real question is how do we narrow our field to the real killer?"

"What does Jake think about our new developments?" Momma asked me.

"I forgot to tell him," I said, feeling at once very foolish for getting so wrapped up in my growing team that I'd neglected to touch base with my husband.

"Shouldn't you do that before we continue?" my mother asked me.

"Excuse me for one second," I said as I stepped into my kitchen and made my call. "Do you have a second, Jake?"

"Just that. What were you doing earlier, leading a parade?"

"What do you mean?"

"I saw you walking across the street from the diner to your donut shop with your mother, Grace, and the mayor himself in tow."

"It appears that we're a team now," I said, explaining to him George's new role in my investigation. "You don't mind, do you?"

"No. As a matter of fact, it will probably do him some good getting involved. I don't know how you're going to keep them all on the same page, though. That's a rough group of rugged individualists. I'll be surprised if you can get them all to agree on anything. Just out of curiosity, why did you recruit George? Didn't you have enough minions as things stood before?"

"They aren't my minions," I said. "We're all equal partners."

"But some of you are more equal than others; I get it. Is that why you called, to get my approval?"

"No, I have a few things to share with you. I don't think Nathaniel or Amber killed Harley."

"Why is that?" The banter went out of his voice, and he was now clearly interested in what I had to say.

"Seth Lancaster basically alibis Nathaniel, and Effie Robbins covers Amber."

After I explained how each was possible, Jake whistled softly. "They're still a little shaky, but I can see how the alibis might hold up. Good work, Suzanne."

"Thank you, sir. How's your investigation coming?" It was a risky question to ask him, but hey, I'd just offered two juicy tidbits to him, so I thought getting an update on his work in turn was fair play. Whether my husband agreed with that conclusion remained to be seen.

"It's coming," he said.

When there was nothing else, I asked, "Can you at least tell me who you're looking at right now?"

"I'd rather not," he said. "After all, it's an open investigation. You understand, don't you?"

I understood, but that didn't mean that I had to like it. I thought of another way of trying to see if we were on the same page. "We're looking at Curtis, Megan, and Wendy. Is there any reason we should drop one of them from our list?"

He paused far too long before he said, "No. Listen, I've got to go."

My husband hung up before I could even thank him, and I considered calling him back, but I knew that would probably be a bad idea. He'd gone beyond his level of comfort, and I knew it, so there was no reason to make it worse. I understood that Jake sometimes told me things about his investigations that he never would have told anyone else, and what was worse, I felt lousy every time I pushed him too far. Would I ever learn, though? It was highly doubtful, because I could never quite see the demarcation of the lines in order not to cross them. I went back to the group to find them having an earnest discussion as to what we should do next.

"What did Jake say?" Grace asked.

"He was pleased to get the information," I said guardedly.

"Did he give you anything in return?" George asked.

"Our marriage isn't quid pro quo," I said firmly.

"Hey, take it easy. I was just asking," George said.

"If you'd like an update, you should ask him yourself," I said, still feeling a little bite of what I'd done. "After all, you're his boss, aren't you?"

"And get my head bit off? No thank you. I may be his superior on paper, but we both know what would happen if I horned in on his case without his permission." George frowned for a moment, and then he asked softly, "I do have his permission, don't I?"

At that moment, he looked like the little boy he must have once been, and I felt myself smiling despite the severity of the situation. "He's fine with it."

"Good," George said with obvious relief. "So, what do we do next?"

"We come up with a plan that helps us trap the real killer without alarming them too much in the process before it's too late."

"How do we go about that?" Grace asked me.

"That's what I'm hoping this brain trust will be able to figure out."

CHAPTER 22

AFTER AN HOUR OF DEBATE, we came up with a plan. Was it the best thing we could do to flush out Harley's killer? I sincerely doubted it, but only time would tell.

"Are you finished with the notes yet?" I asked Grace as she laboriously printed out the message we'd agreed to for the third time.

"This is the last one," she said as she held it up for me to read. "What do you think?"

In block letters that could never be traced back to her hand, the note said, **"I KNOW YOU DID IT AND I HAVE PROOF. TURN YOURSELF IN, OR I WILL!"**

"I love it," I said. I glanced at the clock and said, "We don't have much time to deliver these while our suspects are still at work."

"Let's go then," she said.

I turned to Momma. "Are you sure you want to go with us when we deliver these?"

"I'm a part of this group, Suzanne, and I plan on seeing it out until the end."

"Okay, then. Let's go. I'll ride up front with George, and you and Grace can ride in back, if nobody minds."

"Nobody cares about the seating chart," George said eagerly. "Let's move it."

We all piled into George's black Suburban and headed off to our first suspect's house. The notes might flush out a killer, or they might yield nothing, but at that point, doing something, anything, was better than doing nothing.

"Do you know where everyone lives?" I asked George as we left Donut Hearts.

"No, but while Grace was busy writing those notes, your mother and I looked everyone's addresses up in the phone book. I've already entered them into my GPS, so we're all set."

"Where are we going first?" I asked him, feeling my heart rate begin to increase. It was going to be a little risky dropping off those notes, and after much debate, I'd worn the others down into allowing me to make the deliveries myself. After all, it had been my idea, so it was only fitting that I be the one who took the risks. Once we'd settled on a plan, I'd had an internal debate about whether to tell my husband what we were up to or not.

Ultimately, I'd decided to make the call. After all, long after this case was resolved, I'd have to live with him, so I owed the man that much at least. Was it wrong that I was relieved when my call went straight to voicemail? I'd left a short message telling him that we had a plan and that I'd call him later, and then I'd turned my ringer to silent. At least I'd tried, or so I told myself as I waited for George's answer.

"First up is Megan Gray's house," he said. When we got there, I was relieved to see that her car wasn't in the driveway. Megan lived in a cute little bungalow that couldn't have been more than eight hundred square feet. Though Christmas was long past, there were still lights hanging from the roofline and a deflated plastic Santa lying in a heap in the front yard. I reached back, and Grace handed me the first note, now neatly folded.

I took it from her as Momma said, "Good luck, and be quick."

"I'm not planning on lingering," I said as I got out of the Suburban. I didn't even close the door. Tucking the note into the doorjamb, I rushed back, my heart now beating wildly. It didn't slow until we were on our way to the next house on our list.

"Are you sure I can't do the next one?" Grace asked from the back.

"Thanks, but I've got this. Besides, I need you and Momma to keep a lookout for me from back where you are."

"If you're sure," she said, though she was obviously not convinced of my logic. She was right; I was taking the risk, and there was no room for discussion or debate.

"Next?" I asked George.

He glanced at the GPS. "We're heading to Wendy Crouch's place."

Wendy's home wasn't much larger than Megan's had been, but where the former had been cutely done, this one was in bad need of repair. In place of a front yard, most of the ground had been dug up into an enormous garden, and there was even a small standing greenhouse where I could see plants still thriving inside, despite the frosts and even light snows we'd had. I could see a few tomato plants inside, a row of scallions, and some green bell peppers, all producing lavishly. There was an extension cord running from the house to the greenhouse, where a heater must have kept the space warm enough to extend the growing season this long. Again, I hurried to the door and slipped the note above the doorknob, wedging it into the frame and hoping that it didn't fall out and blow away.

"I never took her for a home gardener," I said when I got back in.

"You never know, do you?" Momma said. "I never saw the point of it, though your grandfather loved his gardens."

"Plural?" I asked.

"Oh, yes. Some were devoted to vegetables, but mostly he grew sunflowers."

"I've seen the pictures," I said. "I just never realized they were his."

"If you'd ever seen him doting on them the way he did, you wouldn't have any question about it. He was quite the hobbyist."

"As interesting as that all is, shouldn't we be heading for Curtis's house?" Grace asked.

"Sorry, I was thinking about something else," George said.

"Anything in particular?" I asked him.

"No, but I'm sure it will come to me. Let's go."

We got to Curtis's house, a nice place in one of April Springs's better neighborhoods, when George pulled up short.

"What's wrong? Is he home?"

"No, but check that out," the mayor said.

I looked where he was pointing and saw that there was a massive amount of discarded things at the curb in front of Curtis Daniels's front yard.

"Is he moving?" Momma asked as she and Grace saw it as well.

"Not that I've heard," I said. "I thought he was gung ho on running the business by himself. Isn't that the impression that you got, Momma?"

"I've heard nothing about him leaving town," she said.

"Should I still put the note by the door?" I asked.

"We might as well follow through, though I suspect we've found our killer," my mother answered.

"Do you really think so?" Grace asked her.

"I'm the least experienced of all of us, but doesn't it seem rather telling that one of our remaining suspects is leaving town so abruptly? Isn't that the very same reason some people believed that you yourself had something to do with Harley's demise, George?"

"It's true enough, as coincidental as it turned out to be," the mayor agreed.

"I'll be right back," I said as I got out, raced toward the

front door, dropped off the note, and then hurried back. On my way back to George's vehicle, I glanced a little closer at the pile. "He's definitely leaving," I said as I got back in and closed the door.

"What makes you so sure?" George asked.

"He's throwing out Christmas decorations, a lawnmower, and a bunch of other equipment that he'd be needing this spring if he were staying. I'm guessing that he's going to be traveling light, wherever he's headed."

"What do we do now?" Momma asked. "I still don't understand this part of it. How will we know if our message has its intended affect?"

"There's just one way to the interstate from all three houses," George said. "Chances are good that whoever's leaving is going to be in a hurry, and they won't be taking back roads. We'll find a place to park on Viewmont Avenue and wait to see who takes the bait. Any ideas on where we should park?"

"Why not beside my building?" I asked.

"Suzanne, Donut Hearts is on Springs Drive," George reminded me.

"I know that," I said. "I'm talking about the old lawyer's offices on Viewmont Avenue."

"You own that?" George asked, clearly surprised.

"My dad left it to me," I said. The words felt odd in my mouth, but it made me kind of proud nonetheless.

"Then that's where we'll wait," George said.

I glanced back at my mother and smiled. She answered with a faint smile of her own. Was that a tear in her eye? I knew that she'd moved on and found love again with Phillip, but a part of her heart would always belong to my father, and there was something about that that gave me great comfort.

George backed the Suburban beside the building where

anyone in a hurry to leave town wouldn't be able to see it, and then we waited.

"What do we do in the meantime?" Grace asked.

"We could go in and check out my place," I said. "Do you have the keys, Momma?"

"Sorry, they're at home," she said.

"That's okay. I can get them later."

"Before the night is out," she promised.

"It's a shame we don't have any playing cards," Grace said.

"Wouldn't it be kind of awkward, given the way we're seated?" Momma asked her.

"We could always play Twenty Questions," I suggested.

"Or perhaps we could just wait silently for something to transpire," Momma answered.

"Okay," Grace said, "but I had a doozy."

"Is it raspberry jam?" I asked her with a smile.

After a moment's silence, Grace asked, "How did you know that?"

"That was the answer you used the last time we played."

"Suzanne, that had to be twenty years ago. How could you possibly remember?" she asked me.

"It's easy. I hold onto the things that are important to me," I said.

"You're one odd bird, you know that, don't you?" George asked good-naturedly beside me.

"Thanks. I'm going to take that as a compliment, considering that it's coming from someone even odder."

"Suzanne," Momma scolded me as if I were little Heather demanding my change.

"Dot, she's right, and what's worse, she knows it. I don't mind being a little odd."

"A little?" Grace asked with a laugh.

"Said the kettle to the pot," George answered.

"I'd resent that remark, if it weren't so true," she answered.

Half a dozen cars passed us as we waited, but none of them belonged to any of our suspects. I was about to give it up as a bad try when a car finally came by that I recognized.

It was kind of hard to miss, given the fact that the acting chief of police for April Springs was driving it, none other than my own dear, sweet husband, Jake.

CHAPTER 23

A**S JAKE APPROACHED MY WINDOW,** I rolled it down and told the others, "Let me do the talking, okay?"

They all agreed, and when Jake got to me, I saw that he wasn't smiling.

"What's going on here?" he asked curtly.

"Can't four friends get together and have a chat without arousing police suspicion?" I asked him with a smile.

Jake wasn't amused. He glanced over at George. "Mayor, I expect this kind of behavior from the three of them, but you used to be a cop yourself. You should know better."

His words cut George deeply; I could see that in one glance at the mayor's expression. "Don't be so hard on him, Jake."

"I'll get to you in a second," he said as he held a hand up in my direction. He was genuinely angry with me, and my blood ran cold feeling his ire. Had I jeopardized my relationship with my husband in my desire to find the same killer he was looking for?

"Well, what do you have to say for yourself?" he asked, turning back to George.

"Jake Bishop, you shouldn't use that tone of voice with your wife, or the mayor, for that matter," Momma said from the back, though in my mind I'd been shouting at her telepathically to keep quiet.

"All due respect, ma'am, but you need to keep your thoughts to yourself until I'm finished here," Jake said.

I glanced back at Momma and saw her face go white. She got

the message, loud and clear, and for once, Grace wasn't smiling either. We'd all managed to land ourselves in some serious hot water with my husband. Once he was satisfied that we weren't going to say anything else, he turned back to George. "I'm still waiting for an answer."

"You know that I don't believe in excuses," George said, "but I got so frustrated with having this cloud of suspicion hanging over me that I had to do something. I'm sorry."

Jake took that in, and then he nodded. "I get that."

"Jake, if it helps, we're all sorry, too," I said.

He frowned for a moment longer, and then he sighed. "Suzanne, I know you're trying to catch Harley's killer too, but you all just about ruined my own plans for catching the person who did it. You might have spooked them with those notes and made it nearly impossible for us to catch them."

"How did you know what we were doing?" I asked him.

"Don't you think I'm working the same list of suspects that you are? I have my people watching all three suspects. The first one radioed me when Curtis found his note, and a minute later, I got the message that Wendy had found hers, too."

"How did they react? Did Megan get hers?" I asked, wondering if our efforts had been for naught.

"We'll never know, because I had my deputy pull her note before she got home. That's how I knew what you four were up to. As to the others, there was nothing other than a quick glance around, and then they both went inside, where they still are, as far as I know. This isn't the way I do business. I'm not about to stand for you mucking into my case this heavy-handedly. I thought we had an agreement."

"I don't know that I violated the letter of it," I said in a weak defense of myself.

"Maybe not, but you sure trampled all over the spirit of it," he replied. After another moment of silence, he looked at George and said, "Mr. Mayor, consider this my formal resignation, effective midnight tonight, whether I manage to unmask the killer or not. Stephen Grant is ready for the job, and frankly, I've had my fill of it."

"Don't be hasty, Jake," George answered. "I said that I was sorry."

"I'm not worried about you so much," he said. "I took this job originally as a favor to the community, but it's not worth the strain it's putting on my marriage."

"Jake, you should at least sleep on it," I said.

"Suzanne, this has been coming for a while, and we both know it," he said tenderly as he reached out and touched my hand lightly. "I don't want to be on opposite sides with you anymore. Is that so hard to understand?"

"No, I get it," I said. I knew my husband well enough to realize that if he said that he was finished, then he was finished. I was just glad that he'd chosen me over working in law enforcement. Then again, that was why he'd left the state police in the first place, in order to be with me.

"Jake, may I say something?" Momma asked softly. I'd nearly forgotten that she was there, she'd been so silent.

"You may," he said. "I'm sorry if I was rough on you."

"You were quite restrained, given the provocation," she said with a smile. "I, too, wanted to add my apologies."

"Me, too," Grace said. "Sorry."

Jake looked at us all steadily, and then he began to smile, which turned into open laughter. "Wow, I didn't realize how much I wanted to quit this job until I actually did it. Suzanne, are you going to be okay having me underfoot all of the time?"

"I'm sure we'll manage just fine," I said with a smile of my own. There had been some additional strain to our relationship since he'd taken over the chief-of-police job, and I realized myself how happy I was that he was quitting. Whatever tomorrow brought, we'd deal with it, together.

"So, what do we do in the meantime?" I asked Jake. "Are you just throwing in the towel?"

"No, I'm going to do my best to wrap this up before midnight," he replied. With a grin, he added, "After all, I'm pretty sure who did it."

"Would you care to share that information with us?" George asked in a humble voice.

"Why not? As long as you all promise to drop this right here and now," Jake said.

We all agreed, given the circumstances. He nodded. "My money is on Curtis Daniels. He had the most to gain by Harley's death, and he had another reason to kill him. I had an accountant friend go through the company's books, and Harley was stealing from him with both hands. It's pretty clear that Curtis found out, and he killed Harley as revenge for stealing the money."

"What about the other two suspects?" I asked.

"I suppose they each are still possibilities, but we'll know soon enough. After I leave here, I'm going to pick Curtis up before he can go on the run, and we're going to have ourselves a nice long talk. He put his house on the market this morning. Didn't you see the junk piled up outside his place?"

"We did," I said. "We thought it was suspicious, too."

He nodded. "Don't worry. I'll have him by midnight. Now, don't you folks have other places to be?"

George started his Suburban as he nodded. "I'll miss having you run things, Jake."

"I'll still be close by, George."

"I'm counting on it," the mayor said, and then he drove us back to the donut shop, where our cars were parked, as Jake went after Curtis Daniels.

"Well, that's that," Momma said. "I have to say, the ending of the case was rather anticlimactic, wasn't it?"

"I'm just glad that no one else got hurt, besides Harley, of course," I said. "As far as I'm concerned, it's a win for the good guys, and that's really all that counts."

"So that's it, then," George said after we all got out. "I'd better go find Grant and tell him the good news. After midnight, he's chief again."

"Not just acting chief this time, right?" Grace asked. "Mayor, it's not fair to keep putting the interim label on him. Either give him the job outright, or find someone else."

"Are you speaking for him now, Grace?" George asked.

"She's right, you know," Momma said. "He's a good man, and he deserves a chance. You heard Jake. He's ready."

"Fine. No qualifiers. Stephen Grant is the new April Springs chief of police come midnight tonight." He looked long and hard at Grace as he added, "Not a word to him before I give him the news, or I'll change my mind and appoint someone else out of sheer spite. Understand?"

"Loud and clear," Grace said.

After the mayor drove away, Momma walked across the street to the diner parking lot where she'd left her car.

I looked at Grace and asked her, "What now? Do you have any plans?"

"No, my evening is suddenly free," she said.

"Why don't you come over and we'll hang out, maybe make something to eat," I suggested. "Our men are going to be tied up most of the night."

"I could cook for us at my place," Grace suggested.

"Really? Since when did you start cooking?"

"Since Stephen told me how much he liked home-cooked meals. Hey, he's made quite a few changes for me. I thought I'd return the favor."

"Will wonders never cease? This is truly a day of miracles," I said.

"I'm not saying that it will be great, but I've gotten pretty good at making stir fry," she said.

"Sold," I answered as we got into my Jeep and drove the short distance to her place.

Once she was in the kitchen prepping our meal, she said, "Suzanne, I'm happy that Stephen is finally getting his promotion, but I hate that it comes at the expense of Jake leaving his job behind."

"Don't worry about that," I said. "He only took the job on a temporary basis. He wouldn't have quit if he hadn't been ready to move on."

"What's he going to do now?" Grace asked as she started chopping up the peppers and onions.

"I don't know. I'm sure between the two of us, we'll figure something out." I could smell the onions as Grace chopped them, and a sudden chill went through me.

I knew who had killed Harley Boggess.

And what was worse, Jake was going after the wrong person.

CHAPTER 24

I CALLED JAKE'S CELLPHONE, BUT HE didn't pick up. Of course. He was probably with Curtis Daniels right now, and he wouldn't allow his time with his suspect to be disturbed by an outside telephone call. "Call Stephen," I ordered Grace.

"You heard George. If I tell him what's about to happen, he might not get the job."

I took the knife from her hand and put it down on the cutting board. "Call him, Grace."

"Okay. What's this about?"

"I'll tell him, and you can listen, too."

There was no answer. The two police officers were probably together. As I held the phone hoping for an answer, there was a knock on the front door, and Grace went to answer it before I could stop her.

"Grace, don't," I said too late.

When the door opened, I saw the killer standing there.

I knew that she'd done it, and what was more, from the look on her face, she knew that I knew.

Light glanced off the steel blade in her hand, and I grabbed the knife Grace had been using and put it into my back pocket, trying not to cut myself in the process. I would have lunged at her with it and ended things one way or the other right then and there, but Grace was between us, and I couldn't put her life in jeopardy.

As she walked in and closed the door behind her, Grace asked, "It was you? You killed Harley?"

"Ask Suzanne," the killer said. "She knows I did it."

Grace looked at me. "Suzanne? Is that true? Why didn't you tell me?"

"I was trying to," I said. "I just figured it out. That's why I was calling Jake and Stephen."

I turned to the killer and said, "You might as well give up now, Wendy. Help is on the way."

"Then I believe I'll stay right where I am," the secretary said. "After all, if you're telling the truth, I could use a hostage, so that gives me one of you to spare."

As she said it, she put her knife to Grace's throat, and I knew that I had to do something, or I was going to be forced to watch my best friend be murdered right in front of me.

CHAPTER 25

"WERE YOU BLACKMAILING HARLEY TO cut you in on what he'd stolen from the company?" I asked, trying to figure out how I could distract Wendy long enough to free Grace from her grasp.

"Is that what you think?" Wendy said with a laugh. "How wrong I was to worry about you and your friends snooping into my life. Harley never stole so much as a postage stamp from that place."

"It was you all along?" I asked, honestly shocked by her admission.

"No one gives the secretary enough credit. I had the passwords and account numbers for both of them, but I realized that Curtis was too sharp for me to steal using his information. Lately Harley's been so distracted that I knew he wouldn't even notice what I was doing."

"Which was?" I asked as I slowly crept closer to them, hoping that Wendy wouldn't notice.

"Systematically gut their bank accounts," she said. "I would have gotten away with it, too, if Amber hadn't convinced Harley to leave the company. I knew that would trigger an audit, and Harley would realize that I'd been duping him. I had to get rid of him before he found out the truth. Once he was unable to refute the accounts, I figured that I'd be in the clear."

"So you killed him. I'm curious, though. Why did you lure him to George's office? It's an odd place to commit murder."

And then I got it. "You knew that it would be empty, didn't you? You're the one who saw him leaving town. I'll bet you called in the anonymous tip that he was fleeing the scene of the crime, too, didn't you?"

"Well, at least you got that right. I figured why not use the information I had to my best ability? I brought this knife to use on him, but I thought George's letter opener sealed the deal, don't you think? It's clear that you knew I was up to something. What gave me away?"

"Onions," I said as I took another small step forward.

"You got that, did you?" she asked. "I was afraid of that happening."

"What about onions?" Grace asked her. "If I'm going to die, I'd at least like to know the truth."

"I'd been picking onions for some soup before I met Harley. I got it all over my hands, but I was inured to the smell by the time I met with him. You smelled it, though, didn't you?"

"I admit, at first I thought he'd had them for lunch. Then, when I saw your greenhouse, I put two and two together."

"That's it? Two coincidences and you believed that I was a killer?"

"There's more. When I first saw you at your office, I thought you were rubbing your hands raw because of Curtis yelling at you, but after you killed Harley, you must have tried to scrub the smell away, in case you left any traces on the handle of the letter opener. I didn't finally put it all together until Grace started cooking. The smell of chopped onions was the trigger, and I knew that you'd done it."

"Very good, though you missed my motive by a mile," she said. "Still, it was a good effort, for an amateur. As much as I've enjoyed our little chat, I'm surprised the police haven't shown up by now. Is there any chance you were lying to me when you told me that you'd called them?"

"If you don't believe me, check my phone," I said as I held it out to her.

She actually lowered the knife a bit as she reached out for my phone with her free hand.

"Now!" I screamed at Grace, who dropped instantly to the ground as though she'd been shot. I didn't have time to pull the knife from my pocket as I dove toward Wendy, driving my body into hers and sending her back against Grace's front door. The knife clattered out of her grip and landed a dozen feet away from us, but her hands weren't empty for long. In a split second, Wendy wrapped them both around my throat and started to squeeze the life out of me.

Grace tried to help, beating her hands against Wendy's head, but she wouldn't release me. The knife I'd tucked in my pocket had sliced through my jeans in the scuffle, and as we finally managed to free Wendy's hands from my throat, she somehow found it. It was heading straight for my back when Grace grabbed the handle just in time, sending it off its direct course to my heart and landing instead in Wendy's side.

She screamed out in pain, and as she reached to pull it out, I grabbed it instead, giving it a little twist on the way out. She was outraged now, a wild animal more than a woman, and I knew that she wouldn't listen to any of our threats or reason. Instead, I pinned her arms while she fought me. "Call 9-1-1," I said breathlessly.

"I'm on it," she said as Wendy kicked furiously at her, doing everything in her power to escape. She couldn't, though. I wasn't going anywhere. She'd come close to ending us both, and I wasn't about to give her another chance at it.

CHAPTER 26

THE NEXT AFTERNOON, WITH STEPHEN Grant duly sworn in as our town's full-fledged chief of police, I had quite a crew working with me at the old law offices my father had left me. Jake was there, newly relieved of his duties and seemingly quite happy about it. Momma and Phillip were helping out as well, and Grace had even taken time out to lend a hand.

"I've never seen so much dust in my life," I said as I wiped down yet another bookshelf.

"I paid the taxes and emergency repairs," Momma said. "I didn't think it needed to be kept pristine."

"I appreciate all you did," I said, and I meant it. I'd gotten over the fact that Momma had hidden my inheritance from me. After all, it had been my father's wish, so how could she not respect it?

"It's the least I can do," she said as she looked around. "What are you going to do with the place? If you'd like to sell it, you can use my agent."

"I thought I might hold onto it," I said. "I know that Teresa Logan is looking for a permanent office, and the extra rent might be nice every month."

"Are you sure you want to do that?" Grace asked. "After all, the woman's got her eye on your husband."

"I'm right here, you know," Jake said. "And besides, that's ridiculous."

"Face it, Jake, some women just can't resist a man in uniform," Phillip said as he smiled at his wife.

"I was attracted to you for other reasons," Momma answered with a grin, which was just about more information than I was interested in.

"It's funny, but all three of us are involved with lawmen," Grace said.

"Correction; that's one lawman, and two that are retired," Jake said.

"How does Stephen like his full title?" I asked Grace.

"He's nervous about letting folks down who believe in him," she said. "I keep telling him that he'll do fine, but I'm not sure he believes me."

"Give him time. He's a good man. He can handle it," Jake answered.

"I'm not worried about him, but I am a little concerned about you," Grace said.

"Why's that?"

"You've done one thing your entire life," Grace said. "And now you've decided not to do it anymore. What does that leave you with?"

It was a question that I'd been contemplating quite a bit over the past eighteen hours myself, but I was glad that I hadn't been the one to ask it.

"Are you kidding? I can do anything I want," he said with a grin. "For the first time in my life, I'm truly free."

My husband looked at me and smiled, and I realized that everything would be all right. We had each other, and whatever came our way next, I knew that we'd face it together, and that was all that I really needed.

RECIPES

A SIMPLE RASPBERRY GLAZE

We've filled donuts with raspberries and whipped cream, an easy recipe that follows below, but for the most raspberry flavor, we like a glaze on a plain donut, whether it be yeast or cake in origin. Basically, this glaze is so good that the donut is simply a delivery device! Depending on how long you simmer the glaze mixture, the flavors will condense and intensify.

Ingredients

- 2 cups raspberries (Fresh is preferred, but frozen will do just fine.)
- 1 cup confectioners' sugar
- 2 teaspoons lemon juice
- 1 teaspoon orange juice

Directions

In a medium-sized saucepan, mix the raspberries (fresh or defrosted if first frozen), powdered sugar, lemon juice, and orange juice. Put the pan over medium heat, stirring often until the raspberries start to release their juices. At that point, raise the heat to medium high and simmer the mixture, stirring occasionally until the mix begins to thicken. This should take anywhere between forty-five seconds and ninety seconds. Remove from heat and strain, pressing the solids down until all of the liquid is extracted. This sauce can be used immediately or refrigerated for up to one week.

Makes enough to drizzle a dozen donuts

Alternate Recipe

You can also skip the steps above and go the easy route, which also happens to be delicious as an added bonus. Put a jar of raspberry preserves into a medium-sized saucepan and heat the mixture over medium heat, stirring occasionally until the preserves start to reduce. As the moisture begins to evaporate, the flavors intensify, and once the mixture takes on your preferred consistency, it can be used immediately or saved in the refrigerator until later.

RASPBERRY-AND-CREAM FILLING

This one relies on an old standard recipe, one that we've used whenever we're in the mood for something light and festive in taste. Again, fresh raspberries are nice, but frozen will do fine once they've been defrosted. It's a nice light touch, and we like this mixture in the summertime when it's hot outside.

Ingredients

- 2 cups whipped cream
- 1 cup raspberries (fresh or frozen), crushed
- 1/2 cup raspberry preserves, jam, or jelly

Directions

This one couldn't be easier. Take the whipped cream and add the preserves along with the crushed raspberries and juice, folding in thoroughly. Using a piping bag or a plastic baggy with one corner snipped off diagonally, pipe this mixture into your favorite whole donut recipe and enjoy. As an added bonus, drizzle with one of the raspberry glaze recipes above for a double shot of raspberry goodness.

PUMPKIN APPLE SPICE DONUTS

These donuts are a bit of an acquired taste, but let's face it, after writing twenty-three donut mysteries and their accompanying recipes, I'm running out of concoctions to create! Some of you have requested recipes featured in the books themselves, so this is my attempt to satisfy your desire—at least of the donut variety! This one was fun to do, so if you're feeling adventurous, have at it. I hope you enjoy the unique flavor combinations, if you're brave enough to try making these yourself!

Ingredients

Mixed

- 2 eggs, beaten
- 3/4 cup fresh apple cider
- 1/4 cup brown sugar, light
- 1/4 cup sugar, white granulated
- 1/4 cup pumpkin pie canned mix

Sifted

- 3–4 cups bread flour
- 1 teaspoon cinnamon

- 1 teaspoon nutmeg
- 1/2 teaspoon baking soda
- 1/2 teaspoon baking powder
- Pinch of salt
- 2 tablespoons butter, salted, melted and at room temperature
- Canola oil, enough for frying the donuts

Directions

Heat the oil to 360 degrees F.

While you're waiting for the oil to reach the proper temperature, take a medium-sized bowl, add the beaten eggs and cider together, and then loosely incorporate them. Next, add the brown sugar, granulated sugar, and pumpkin pie mix to this blend, again incorporating thoroughly.

In a separate medium-sized bowl, mix the flour, cinnamon, nutmeg, baking soda, baking powder, and salt together until it's thoroughly blended. Mix this together, adding the melted butter last. If the dough is too sticky to work properly, add small increments of flour until you get a consistency you like. If you add too much flour, add a little more cider until you get the perfect dough. Roll the dough out 1/2 to 1/4 inch thick, then cut out the donut shapes using a cutter or a water glass. Fry the donut rounds in canola oil for 3 to 4 minutes, turning halfway when one side is golden brown. These can be coated with confectioners' sugar after frying or lightly coated with apple butter.

Makes six to twelve donuts.

If you enjoy Jessica Beck Mysteries and you would like to be notified when the next book is being released, please send your email address to newreleases@jessicabeckmysteries.net. Your email address will not be shared, sold, bartered, traded, broadcast, or disclosed in any way. There will be no spam from us, just a friendly reminder when the latest book is being released.

Also, be sure to visit our website at jessicabeckmysteries.net for valuable information about Jessica's books.

OTHER BOOKS BY JESSICA BECK

Printed in Great Britain
by Amazon